11

UNDERGROUND
IN OCEAN ALLEY

ELAINE L. ORR

ISBN: 978-1-948070-09-6
Library of Congress Preassigned Number:

DEDICATION

To the next generation: Ellie, Sadie, Grayson, Peyton, and Caitlin. May they all love to read.

Elaine L. Orr

ACKNOWLEDGMENTS

With thanks to the Decatur Critique Group – Angela,
Dave, Debbie, Marilyn, and both Sues.

CHAPTER ONE

I'VE GOTTEN USED TO people asking about our three-year old twins Lance and Leah. They are cut-ups, of course, but they are best known for their chaotic births.

I knew when my water broke that Scoobie and I needed to hustle to Ocean Alley's Hospital. My smart husband credits a sixth sense for calling an ambulance to take us there. He says my expression was akin to a mix of bad gas and a hard kick to the kidney.

In any event, Lance was born in the ambulance and Leah just inside the emergency room entrance. Better than the lobby, I suppose.

Aunt Madge says the heavens looked upon us kindly, and Scoobie's best friend George wishes he had organized a pool to wager on the time between first pain and first baby.

Three years later, afternoons are about the only quiet time I get. The twins take a nap, bread dough is ready to go into the oven, and Cozy Corner B&B guests are about town or in their rooms. I don't nap but I close my eyes.

The sharp rap on the front door jerked me awake. For a second I wasn't sure whether I was in the B&B or Scoobie's and my place. Home, I was home. So the person at the door would likely be someone I knew. I didn't bother to check my hair in the hall mirror.

A glance out the peep hole showed the buds that had turned to light green leaves on our maple tree, and a familiar shape. I opened the door. "Sergeant Morehouse. Haven't seen you in ages."

"You musta been behaving, Jolie."

I stood aside so he could enter, and quietly closed the door. "Twins are sleeping. They just…" I took in the bags under his eyes and haggard expression. He looked older than his forty-odd years. "Are you sick?"

"No." He's been in our living room many times, so he settled himself on the sofa and gestured that I should sit near him.

Any other time I'd have thought this presumptuous behavior in my own home, but today I could tell something had him on edge. "What's up?"

"I'm looking for Kevin."

"Gee, now that the boys are in high school, we mostly only see him at track practice."

He nodded. "Yeah, I thought Terry mighta heard from him."

"Heard from him? Where is he?"

"I don't know."

"But, your sister knows, right?" Morehouse spent a lot of time with his two nephews, and Scoobie's much younger brother Terry was close to Kevin. At Morehouse's request, Kevin, a year older than Terry, had introduced Terry to other kids in middle school when the death of their father brought Terry to Scoobie and me four years ago.

"She's worried sick. His bed was empty this morning, and he didn't show up at school."

A soft grunt from the baby monitor drew our attention, but when nothing else followed I looked back at Morehouse. "Kevin wouldn't run away would he? I mean, he's never been in trouble or anything."

Morehouse ran a hand through his closely cropped hair and stood to pace our long living room. "He's been moody since that emergency appendectomy a couple months ago. We thought maybe some effect from the anesthesia."

I nodded slowly. "I saw him throw the baton when he missed handing it off in the relay a couple weeks ago, but I guess I don't see him enough to have noticed moodiness."

Morehouse's phone beeped and he read a message. "Huh. You know Sandra Cartwright at the hospital?"

"Friend of Aunt Madge's. Director of nursing." And also attended Aunt Madge and Harry's church, First Presbyterian, or First Prez as it's called. She also helped a few times at Harvest for All Food Pantry, which is located at the church.

"Yeah. Looks like she maybe had a heart attack yesterday, then fell and hit her head. Madge is all over town these days. Did she hear about it?"

"I think she would have called. Sorry to hear."

He studied the message. "Our guys did a wellness check. Her day off yesterday, so no one had looked."

Ugh. "She always looked so healthy. She wasn't even sixty was she?"

Morehouse shook his head. "Probably about that. Too damn bad." He stuffed his phone in the pocket of his polyester pants. "But no need for police, so I gotta get back to the station to get the guys to help me put up signs. I'm hopin' the chief'll authorize an Amber Alert."

"Doesn't there have to be an indication of potential harm…" I stopped. "I'll help put up signs. I can take the kids in the stroller to the boardwalk, and go in all the businesses."

He smiled slightly. "All that stroller walking. No one would know you got kids if you weren't pushing 'em."

I took that as a compliment that I didn't look my thirty-four years. My five-foot-three frame actually looks more fit than before the kids. "Thanks."

He turned to leave. Over his shoulder, he said, "Ask Terry to call me, would you?"

"Sure." I stayed seated, and Morehouse remembered not to bang the door as he left.

As I thought about it, I vaguely recalled Terry telling Scoobie that Kevin had been a butt-head about something, but I didn't know what the issue was. I gazed around our cozy living room and tried to imagine our house if Terry were suddenly gone. I shivered.

Maybe Kevin was out of sorts about his grades or a girl. Surely he would be back soon.

When in doubt, I call Aunt Madge. Now that she's running for mayor of Ocean Alley, she is all over our two-mile long, twelve-block deep town. I'm trying to bother her less.

As I listened to her phone ring, I remembered that she and her husband-campaign-manager Harry had several meetings Monday afternoon, including at Silver Times Senior Living. She said if she couldn't grab the senior vote she didn't stand a chance of winning.

I smiled as I thought of her campaign slogan: *Madge for Mayor: Let Experience Speak for You*. Scoobie altered two of her signs to say: *Madge for Boss: Do What She Says*. They are under other signs in a pile on her coffee table, so she hasn't seen them yet.

My call went to voice mail. "Just saying hello. And Sergeant Morehouse says to keep an eye out for his nephew Kevin. He's…" I didn't want to say missing. "He's upset about something. You don't need to call me unless you see him." I hung up without mentioning Sandra Cartwright. Better to relay that news in person, or at least on the phone rather than in a message.

I sent a quick email about Kevin and Sandra Cartwright to Megan, who volunteers with Scoobie and me a lot at the food pantry. Since Megan also runs Java Jolt coffee shop, she would be able to let others know about finding Kevin and remembering Sandra.

At the end of the email, I asked her to let Max know. He loves to assist almost anyone, and helps Megan empty trash and such at Java Jolt, a form of thanks for the broken pastry pieces she supplies him with.

The always-good-natured Max sustained a TBI during the Iraq War. He has become part of our network of friends, not a friend I would have expected to have, and one whose repetitive speech patterns sometimes confuse the twins.

I glanced at the clock on the mantle above our fireplace. At roughly three-fifteen, Scoobie would arrive home after work in the hospital's Radiology Department. I'd head next door to the Cozy Corner to put the two loaves of bread, already rising, into Aunt Madge's oven.

Sandra's death would hit the hospital hard at any time, but especially now. In a tourist town like Ocean Alley, the hospital is busiest during the peak season. At the Jersey shore that's summer, so the hospital was gearing up.

Scoobie had mentioned the hospital inpatient census was especially low this winter. That meant less income and reduced hours for some staff. So far, Scoobie hadn't been affected. But some people grumbled, and Sandra had a gift for calming staff as well as patients.

I took a few minutes to put lunch cutlery in the dishwasher and toss trucks and balls into the toy box at the far end of the living room. If someone had told me four years ago that Scoobie and I would not only be married but the parents of three-year old twins, I'd have scoffed at the idea. Or freaked out.

When we looked for a new house before the twins were born, we'd been thrilled to find the large Cape Cod cottage, on D Street next to the B&B, on the market. Our friend Lester Argrow, the most annoying real estate agent in Ocean Alley, knew we were looking and persuaded the couple who owned it to sell a year earlier than they planned.

He told us he'd informed them he foresaw a dip in home prices. Apparently he also implied Aunt Madge was ill, because when we moved in they pronounced her recovery "miraculous." I never bothered to ask Lester what they meant.

The front door opened and Scoobie came into the kitchen and kissed my cheek. "Hello, Domestic Goddess."

"Very Funny." I kissed him on the lips. An afternoon kiss, not a bedtime kiss. "Kids are still sleeping."

He grabbed a banana from a bowl on the kitchen table. "How's Leah's cold?"

"Much better, but I'm starting to think Lance might be coming down with it."

He mimicked my mother's tone of voice. "You need to get those children on a schedule."

I threw the sponge at him. "I think they're coming for Thanksgiving."

Scoobie simply nodded. My mother is a thorn in anyone's side, but his mother had been more or less evil incarnate. I try to be grateful for my parents' interest in the twins. And be glad she and Dad live in Florida.

I opened the fridge and took out apple juice to fill the twins' sippy cups. "Sergeant Morehouse came by. He…"

"What did you do?"

I looked at Scoobie, half in irritation, and had to smile when he wiggled his eyebrows at me. "He had a serious request." I relayed the information about Kevin, then remembered to add the sad news about Sandra Cartwright.

Scoobie sank onto a chair near the kitchen table. "Gee. No word on Sandra at the hospital before I left for home."

"Morehouse got a text while he was here. He said something about no one having checked earlier because yesterday was her day off."

Scoobie squared his shoulders. "Damned shame, but let's focus on Kevin first. Terry was irritated at him the other day. Something about Kevin missing track practice and Terry having to time the other runners for the coach."

I tightened the lid on Lance's cup. He's managed to unscrew it a few times. "I wouldn't think that translated into running away."

Scoobie tossed the banana peel into the trash can under the sink. "But if Morehouse doesn't think Kevin would just hoof it, something's going on. When the twins wake up, I'll load them in the Odyssey and we can watch track practice. Maybe I'll pick up something."

The monitor announced that Leah was awake. "Gotta get to the Cozy Corner." I blew Scoobie a kiss. "Have fun, Daddy."

And he would.

I half jogged from our wide front porch to the wrap-around one on the three-story Victorian B&B. Aunt Madge bought it thirty years ago, just after Uncle Gordon died. She repaints it a soft blue with white trim every few years, and her carpentry skills keep it in great shape. Since Harry moved from his place to hers, she has a helper.

I keyed in the code on the pad at the outside door, which opens into a small hallway near the guests' breakfast room. George added the keypad to Aunt Madge's security system a couple of years ago. She loves it. She tells guests the code and then changes it weekly.

Aunt Madge has the only B&B in town that provides an afternoon snack, which partially explains why the B&B is as busy as she wants it to be. Which sometimes is not busy at all. I noticed yesterday that her calendar showed the week before the upcoming municipal election as a time not to accept any more guests.

I turned on the Tiffany lamp on the sideboard, just outside the great room. I would serve the hot bread – plain and cheddar cheese – on it, along with the tea. Sitting next to the lamp was a framed photo of Aunt Madge's dogs, Mister Rogers and Miss Piggy. My black cat, Jazz, sat on Mister Rogers' back.

When I first moved into the B&B seven years ago, Jazz terrified the dogs. Now they can't get enough of each other. But the dogs are old, roughly ten. Aunt Madge adopted the exuberant retrievers from the local shelter, so their ages are estimates.

The twins use the dogs as pillows when they play in Aunt Madge's great room. I dread the thought of one of them passing.

I walked through the swinging door that separates the guests' breakfast room from Aunt Madge and Harry's living space. Their great room, a combined kitchen and living room, is my favorite place on earth. Scoobie would not be jealous. He loves to be here, too.

The pecan cabinetry and butcher-block countertops are relatively new, and blend well with the oak table and antique ice box. Kind of like Aunt Madge. A perfect mix of old and innovative.

The great room opens onto the back deck. I felt chilly. The thermostat showed sixty-five, so I switched on the heat before turning on the oven.

A glance out the sliding glass door showed the dogs curled into each other on a large bean-bag bed on the back porch. Aunt Madge and I coordinate their trips outside during her campaign.

I went to the counter to peer under the towel covering the rising dough. Terry, a much better cook than I, likes to punch it down and put it in the bread pans to bake. But he wouldn't be home in time today.

However, three minutes later he charged into the great room, dropped his backpack on the floor, and stared at me. "Kevin is missing!"

I pointed at the large oak table. "His uncle told me. Sit."

He glanced at the counter. "I can punch the bread while we talk." He walked to the sink and began to wash his hands.

"Scoobie was going to go to track practice to see if there was news, but I gather it's been called off?"

He dried his hands and pulled the bowl to him. "Yeah. We're spreading out to see if we can find him. I wanted to tell you guys and then I'm going into the Popsicle District to walk the streets."

I studied his handsome, fifteen-year old profile. Except that he lacks a beard and has brown hair rather than blonde like Scoobie, the brothers look much alike. Well, half-brothers, but we've never used the term.

Terry arrived, not merely unannounced but unknown, on our wedding night four years ago. Life changed forever.

We'd expected to be parents in a few months, but the addition of a grieving ten-year old gave us instant experience. He's more like a son to us than brother or brother-in-law. The twins call him their brother, in large part because Terry announced he didn't want to be called uncle. We'll eventually sort it out for them.

They recently asked why Scoobie and Terry have the last name O'Brien, and mine is Gentil. I kept my family name because neither my parents or my dad's brother had sons. The name would be gone if I didn't keep it.

Gentil means nice in French and Jolie means pretty. Clearly my dad's French Canadian ancestry was in full bloom when he suggested the name for his second daughter. Or, as Scoobie says, he could have been smoking something.

Terry hit the rising dough as if it was a punching bag. "The thing is, I knew something was bothering him. I asked him a bunch of times. Last time he told me to F off, and I've hardly talked to him for a week."

I took plates from a cabinet. "You don't feel guilty do you?"

His shoulders bent forward. "Kinda do."

"Don't. He made his choice for some reason that made sense to him. We'll help find him and bring him home." I said this with more confidence than I felt. If Kevin had left the night before, he'd have a big head start. "Did he take his car?"

Terry shook his head. "That's why we're looking in town." He placed the two loaves into baking pans and then the oven.

Something occurred to me. "How did you get here if Kevin didn't drop you off?"

He picked up his backpack and walked with me into the breakfast room. "I'm gonna jog over to the Popsicle District. Can I call you guys for a ride back?"

"Sure. Wait. Call Scoobie. He may have already loaded the Odyssey to take the twins to the high school. He can pick you up and drive you to the Popsicle District. There's a stroller in the van."

It registered that Terry had not answered my question about a ride home, but I decided not to push it. He pulled out his phone and punched the number for Scoobie as he walked out of the Cozy Corner.

I could envision him walking through the neighborhood of multi-colored bungalows, peering into yards and the occasional vacant house. In early May, most summer cottages had not opened for the season. Better to have Scoobie and the twins with him than someone call to report a burglar.

I spent the next hour setting up for the afternoon snack, wiping my kids' fingerprints off the sliding glass door in the great room, and letting the dogs in and out to play in the small back yard. In between tasks, I made a final to-do list for the Harvest for All fundraiser, which would take place on the boardwalk in a few days.

For the first time, we had a Cinco de Mayo theme. Megan's daughter Alicia has Hispanic heritage through her father, and over the winter she teased me about the Mexicans defeating the French attack in 1862. Scoobie chimed in and said she could put her cultural pride to work and help us plan the next fundraiser around a Cinco de Mayo theme.

At first I thought the idea could be too ambitious. We go in nine directions the week before a fundraiser, and that's without having to be sure to line up Spanish-language entertainment and costumes. Wrong. Other towns have the festivals, and people seemed excited to have one here. The high school Spanish Club and band stepped up to plan festive dancing and decorations.

More than half the boardwalk merchants planned to open this weekend for the Cinco de Mayo fundraiser, and would donate some of what they made to the pantry. They would also collect canned goods. For the business that secured the most, Harvest for All would make and distribute a poster with a thank-you photo of them and their goodies.

We had finally gotten permission to use the kiddie rides area for games, which people would donate to play. The crowning activity would be the piñata game. We'd had one at a Halloween fundraiser a few years ago, but I'd been distracted by a kidnapping. This piñata swatting should go more smoothly.

The dinging timer announced the bread had finished baking. I sliced half of each loaf on a cutting board and carried the results into the breakfast room.

First to follow the wonderful smell to the room was Bart Mobley. He and his now late wife stayed at the B&B every fall, usually for two weeks. He grew up in Ocean Alley in the 1940s and can wax nostalgic for half-an-hour, which he does more often in the two years since his wife died.

Bart helped himself to a slice of each type of bread. "So, Jolie, how's her campaign going?"

I shrugged. "As Harry says, they're having a good time. They sure work hard."

"I don't like the idea of a year-round resort either. I'm glad she wants to keep the town the same."

I chose my words carefully. Aunt Madge is progressive, and believes a larger hotel would breathe life into town – and her business. She does not want the nine-story resort, especially since the developer also built a couple of casinos south of Ocean Alley. She thinks if they got a toehold in town that they'd try to get a casino eventually. Ocean Alley would never be the same. I agree with her.

"She likes the idea of more people spending time here. But she and Harry don't want clogged streets and mini-conventions, which the developer wants to host."

Bart dabbed at a drop of jam on his pants, and I squirted a napkin with hot water from the tea jug and handed it to him.

He nodded thanks. "I mind as how people in town thought Beachcomber's Alley was too big when it got renovated in, oh, maybe the 1960s. Course now that hotel seems small. Get a huge resort thing and you'll have to maybe add onto the schools, maybe even the hospital."

I figured Bart probably knew Sandra. Better I should share the sad news than he heard it elsewhere. "Did you know Sandra Cartwright at the hospital?"

He glanced up from his spot dabbing. "Sounds like you're going to tell me Sandra died."

"I'm afraid so. I heard maybe a heart attack at home, probably yesterday."

"Well, dang. She dated my younger cousin when they were in high school. Guess I better call him."

The other three guests came in, and I busied myself with keeping the coffee and tea thermoses full and trying to remember what I'd heard about a new restaurant on the edge of town. They planned to try it for dinner.

When the guests had returned to their rooms or, in Bart's case to find a book on a shelf in the guest living room, I loaded Aunt Madge's dishwasher and wiped off the breakfast room tables.

Crunching gravel and barks of Mister Rogers and Miss Piggy from the back yard announced our Odyssey. I dried my hands and opened the side door.

Terry launched himself from the front passenger seat holding what looked like a green army blanket. Scoobie got out of the driver's side and slid open the side door to get the kids. He shook his head and shrugged at me before he leaned into the van.

Terry bounded up the steps and through the screen door. "I found his coat. It was on the ground near a bus stop in the Popsicle District." He thrust it at me as he barged into the hall. "Is that dark spot on the sleeve blood?"

CHAPTER TWO

I LET THE COAT FALL to the floor.

He stooped to pick it up. "Why'd you do that?"

I spoke harshly. "Don't touch it again."

He straightened, and probably would have been angry if he hadn't been so surprised.

I touched his arm. "Sorry. We'll call his uncle. Maybe someone else's fingerprints are on it. Why don't you help Scoobie while I call Sergeant Morehouse?"

Morehouse practically spat his greeting. "What?"

"Terry thinks he found Kevin's coat, and…"

"Where the hell did he find it, and where is it?"

I avoided telling him to let me finish a sentence. "By a bus stop in the Popsicle District. He brought it here."

Morehouse hung up without saying good-bye, his usual way to end a call.

I opened the screen door and reached out to take Leah from Scoobie. She looked as if she'd had a ten-minute nap in the van. She's usually cranky after those, so I gave her my biggest smile. "Hello pretty girl."

Scoobie kissed me as she buried her snotty nose in my shoulder. He handed me a Kleenex. "Never-ending battle."

Terry came toward the B&B's small side porch, holding Lance's hand. He let our more stubborn twin count each of the four steps as they landed on them.

I glanced back at Scoobie. "I called Morehouse, but I'm not sure if he'll come here or our place."

"He'll see the Odyssey. He knows you come here in the afternoons a lot of days."

Terry bent over to pretend he was grabbing Lance's nose, but he spoke to Scoobie. "When we get Jolie and the kids back to our place, can you drive me to the police station? I want to see what's going on."

I answered for Scoobie, which he hates. "Sergeant Morehouse is coming by here in a minute, for the jacket."

Scoobie took Leah from me, removed her coat, and opened the sideboard to retrieve her brown stuffed bear. He placed her and the bear on the floor, and reached in to get Lance's stuffed cat. "You guys can go look out the back window at the dogs."

They raced each other through the swinging door into the great room, and Scoobie, Terry, and I looked at each other.

Terry spoke first. "The coat must mean something really bad happened to him."

Scoobie used his comforting-a-patient tone. "Or that he took a heavier coat than he needed and forgot he set it down."

"But the blood…" Terry began.

Tires squealed into the Cozy Corner parking lot. Morehouse exited his dark green Chevy Caprice and rushed up Aunt Madge's side steps. Scoobie opened the door for him.

He barely acknowledged Scoobie and me, and walked to Terry. "Did you see him? Did he say where he was going?"

Terry shook his head. "No. I'm sorry. Do you know why he was so ticked off lately?"

I gestured to the grouping of small tables in the breakfast room. "Sit, Sergeant. Do you want tea while we talk? It's still hot."

His impatient wave said he wanted no tea and preferred to keep standing, but he sat. "He's seemed kind of jittery since the operation. He was in there a few days because the appendix almost ruptured, and he had that infection."

Terry sat across from Morehouse and Scoobie and I sat at the next table.

Terry frowned. "He didn't want to be in there that long. I thought last week maybe he didn't feel good. I saw him in Java Jolt last Sunday, talking to that nurse. The older one. She…"

Scoobie, Morehouse and I said, "Sandra Cartwright?" Morehouse's question was more like a bellow.

Terry leaned back in his chair. "She's helping on Aunt Madge's campaign."

"I forgot she was helping," I began.

Morehouse interrupted me. "What were they talking about? You saw 'em. You musta heard 'em."

In an even tone, Scoobie said, "He'll tell you."

Morehouse nodded.

Terry shook his head. "I don't know. She was in there, you know, after church, and I was helping Megan for a couple hours, like I always do on Sunday."

Morehouse took a slow breath. "You think he went there to talk to her?"

Terry weighed the question. "I don't know. Kevin comes by a lot of Sundays when I work, so he could have figured she would be there. She comes a lot."

Morehouse looked at me. "Does he know?"

I shook my head. "Terry, Sandra Cartwright seems to have had a heart attack."

"Is she okay?"

"No." Morehouse said.

Scoobie put a hand on Terry's shoulder. "I'm afraid she passed."

Morehouse stood. "Where's that coat? I'm gonna take it with me and check out Sandra's place."

"I liked her." Terry said. "She came to middle school to do a talk on flu vaccines."

I moved toward the kitchen. "I'll get a big bag for the coat." I wanted to check on the twins. The great room was too quiet.

I walked into the kitchen end of the great room and observed the backs of two blonde heads as the twins pressed their tongues against the sliding glass door – apparently to amuse the dogs. I ignored the transgression so I could grab a trash bag and get back to the breakfast room. *Thank heavens I just cleaned that door.*

When I got back to the breakfast room twenty seconds later, Scoobie and Terry were talking quietly at a table and Morehouse was fixated on a text. "Do you want me to put it in the bag for you?"

He looked up, grabbed a cloth napkin from a table, and leaned over to pick the coat off the floor. "Not likely prints, but you never know." He stuffed the coat in the white plastic bag that I held open for him.

Terry stood. "What about the blood?"

"What blood?" Morehouse asked.

I answered. "It's on the right cuff. Maybe two square inches."

Morehouse used the napkin to take the coat out of the bag and regarded the sleeve.

"Is it just on the outside?" I asked.

Morehouse pulled the cuff back a little. "Inside, too."

"Could have soaked through," Scoobie said.

"If it soaked through from the outside, does that mean it's someone else's blood?" I asked.

The kitchen door swung open, and Leah said, "Lance wants to go outside."

Scoobie walked to her and the two went into the kitchen, door swinging shut behind them. "We're going back to our house in a minute. You and Lance need to stay inside."

Morehouse put the coat back in the bag. "Could mean anything." He studied Terry. "Anyone else I should talk to at school?"

"You talked to the track coach, right?"

"Mr. Griffin. Yeah. He'll get with a bunch of people and call me."

Terry did a small shrug. "He used to date Cathy Giacomo, but she might be mad at him, too."

Morehouse nodded his head as he walked to the door. "I talked to her. Don't know what's gotten into that kid."

I shut the door behind Morehouse and regarded Terry. "He's only been different since the appendectomy?"

"Worse since Sunday. I wonder if it has anything to do with what he and Ms. Cartwright talked about?"

"Seems unlikely, but it's worth thinking about, I guess. Why don't you and Scoobie drive around some more? And stop by the station. Morehouse said he was going to make some signs to post."

I HAD FED LANCE AND LEAH and parted the curtains at the front window of our house five times when Aunt Madge called. "What's this about Kevin?"

I realized she couldn't have heard about Sandra Cartwright. She might ask about Kevin first, but I would have heard the grief in her tone. "He wasn't in his bed this morning and didn't go to school. Morehouse came over to talk to us, and Scoobie and Terry are driving around."

"Hmm." She paused for several seconds. "There is one person I can ask.'

"Uh, Aunt Madge, is it your friend Sandra?"

"How did you know that?"

I was itching to ask what she thought Sandra might know, but did the right thing. "I'm sorry, but she seems to have had a heart attack. She passed."

Aunt Madge's tone grew irritable. "Why can't people just say someone died? Was she at work?"

"Home, I believe. She had a day off yesterday.'

"Oh, dear. If she had been at work maybe someone could have helped her." Her voice grew quieter as she moved the phone away from her mouth. "Harry. Jolie said Sandra Cartwright died." Her voice caught on the word died.

Harry came on the line. "We're sorry to hear that, Jolie. We were at the Chamber of Commerce for a couple of hours. Surprised we didn't hear."

"Morehouse only found out about the same time."

"Are they investigating something?" Harry asked.

"He said something about not police business."

Aunt Madge came back on the phone. "I should call the sergeant. Sandra has spoken to Kevin several times lately. Though I'm not sure about what."

I checked myself before I said it was too late to find out. "Okay, I'll call you if we hear anything about Kevin."

As she started to say goodbye, I asked, "Oh. Did the Chamber endorse you?"

She blew her lips together as if disgusted. "Not on a bet. The director has been telling people I'm against progress. I thought if we met I could explain I simply don't want such a huge project. I asked them if the developer was going to pay to widen the road around the new hotel, and it turns out they're going to pay him to come here."

"You mean, like under the table?"

"No." She laughed. "A tax incentive. We'll all pay for that monstrosity for years. I suggested if we were going spend city money, we could give some incentives to the hotels that are already in business. They've paid taxes here for years, and that bozo…"

Harry called to her. "Honey, are you ready to eat?"

I stifled a laugh. Harry had probably heard these themes many times. "Tell Harry I'm appraising that place on Conch tomorrow."

"I will. Kiss the twins for me."

I hung up and regarded them. Lance had his head halfway under our fairly new navy blue couch, which meant Jazz was under there. Leah sat behind a large potted plant, which indicated she was up to something.

I peered behind the plant and groaned. "Where did you get that lipstick?"

She beamed at me, red line on her face from cheek to cheek. "Mommy's purse."

Lance pulled out from under the couch. "I helped."

CHAPTER THREE

AFTER AN EXHAUSTED Terry said he would get up early to do math homework, Scoobie walked him upstairs. The pre-bed conversation is their regular brother bonding time.

I texted Morehouse to ask if I could pick up flyers in the morning, and he texted back. "Stop by at seven-thirty."

I replied that I would be there after I dropped the kids off at daycare, about eight-fifteen. It felt strange to have him ask for my help, and I was itching to do something. In the BT Era (before twins) I would have roamed the streets this evening. Probably a bunch of people were doing that, friends of Kevin's who would have a better idea of where he might hide.

Assuming he was hiding and not hurt.

Scoobie came down the steps and together we plopped on the couch. "I'd take off tomorrow, but my colleague Gina has a dentist appointment to get wisdom teeth pulled. I really need to be there."

I nodded. "Morehouse asked me to stop by to get some signs. I said I'd do it after I drop off the kids. But then I have to appraise a house."

"At least you'll be around town. You can ask people."

Jazz joined us. When the twins were born, we decided to give away her playmate, a de-scented pet skunk I'd inherited from the woman who owned our prior home before I bought it. We found her a great spot at a petting zoo in Asbury Park, and Scoobie took Jazz to visit Pebbles a couple of times. Pebbles was her usual nonplussed self, and once Jazz knew where she was, Jazz stopped searching the house for her.

We took the twins once, but they wanted to bring Pebbles home, so we won't do that again.

Jazz walked across the back of the sofa and ended up in Scoobie's lap. I reached over to stroke her head. "Aunt Madge said that Kevin had talked to Sandra Cartwright a few times, but she didn't really know why."

Scoobie frowned. "Maybe Kevin had some complaints about when he was in the hospital."

"You don't suppose…" I stopped.

"What?"

"Do you think that could be Sandra's blood on Kevin's coat?"

Scoobie grimaced. "Not sure she would have been bleeding after a heart attack. And why would he be at her house? "

"Maybe she hit her head."

He tugged at my hair, which hung in brown clumps after a long day. "You can ask Morehouse, but if I were you, I wouldn't give him a reason to be more upset."

TUESDAY MORNING, I HAD TO explain to Natalie, the daycare teacher, why Leah had red lines on her face.

Natalie smiled. "I'll try a spot of baby oil on a baby wipe, if you want."

"That would be great. I tried a wipe and she told me the lipstick was on her face not her bottom."

She grinned. "I won't let her see me take it out of the baby wipe tub."

The police station is in the heart of downtown Ocean Alley, to use the term loosely. While not a town square in the true sense, the block that houses the station also has the court house, post office, library, and small in-town grocery. It is as close to a business district as a small beach town can get.

I took two minutes to drive to the station and walked to the counter. When I could tell the young officer would be several minutes helping a woman who came in to report graffiti on her sidewalk, I sat in one of the plastic chairs and texted Morehouse.

He replied that he would be out in three minutes. I stared around the reception area. Behind the counter are a couple of desks, usually empty, and a bunch of cubbyholes for mail. A locked entrance to the bullpen and offices is to the right of the counter.

The bulletin board, next to the chair I sat in, bore the kinds of signs seen in post offices – photos of unsmiling criminals. It also held announcements of bake sales or car washes, and one about the food pantry Cinco de Mayo fundraiser this weekend.

Today, a prominent poster had Kevin's photo and description: five feet seven inches tall, one hundred ten pounds, black hair, dark brown eyes, and a recent abdominal scar. It also noted he might be wearing a blue jeans jacket and dark colored pants.

A buzzer on the right announced Morehouse. He waved me toward him and held open the door to the offices until I was through it. His appearance was almost shockingly haggard and his brown slacks looked as if he had slept in them.

"Any news?" I asked.

"Nuthin'. Come on back."

I followed him to his tiny office, which boasts two file cabinets, his desk, and a couple of wooden visitor chairs. Not enough unused floor space to spread a beach towel.

He sank into his desk chair and regarded me. "I been told to be careful how much time I spend lookin' for Kevin."

"What? He's missing!"

Morehouse nodded. "Yeah. But no signs of foul play, and he ain't been gone long. If he was someone else's kid, we wouldn't be doing a lot yet."

I thought about that. "On TV shows they tell parents that and then they find the kid's body."

Morehouse's expression went blank.

"Oh, crud. I'm sorry."

"Plenty of real-world cases like that. My sister is crazed with worry."

"Can you take leave to look?"

He nodded. "I been debatin' it. Thing is, nobody's going to give me grief for watching incomin' info from nearby towns or making a few phone calls. I think I learn more by being here."

"How can I help?"

"First, keep your ears open around Terry. You think he would tell you if he knows anything?"

"He talks to us pretty easily. Especially Scoobie."

"Okay. I never thought I'd say this, but I want you to get together with George, and Scoobie of course, and search for him. None of you look like cops. And Scoobie can keep an eye out at the hospital, too."

"Of course." Before I could say more, his phone buzzed.

He picked up the receiver. "Yes?"

I could hear the front desk officer's voice. "Sergeant, there's a guy here who insists…"

A man's voice yelled, "Tell him it's Lester. I'm here to help him find the kid."

Morehouse half-smiled as he spoke to the officer. "He goes all over town. I'll come out and get him." He hung up, stood, and looked at me. "You want a partner?"

Lester has the finesse of a sea lion on a school bus. "He is, uh, persistent."

Morehouse grunted and walked out.

I picked up one of the flyers from a stack on his desk and reread it. What would make Kevin not only leave but stay away? He had to know his mother would be frantic.

Lester's voice preceded him and Morehouse. For a short Italian, he projects like a lumberjack. "See, I been thinkin'. We do a search by grid. And we focus a lot on empty houses."

Morehouse walked in, and Lester stopped in the doorway. "I just called your house, Jolie. Figured you hadn't left to appraise the house on Conch."

Morehouse sat. "If you got work, Jolie."

I turned from Lester to face him. "It'll only take an hour or so. I can search for Kevin before and after."

Lester picked up a stack of the flyers. "I'll give a bunch to Ramona at her gallery."

Lester is only ten years older than his niece, Ramona, my good friend. A few months ago she left her job at the Purple Cow, the local office supply store, and opened an art gallery. She features her own watercolors and pen-and-ink drawings, as well as other artists' work. She also teaches various art classes. For the twins' last birthday, she did a great pen-and-ink sketch of them.

Morehouse nodded. "I keep forgettin' she's not at the other place. I was going to ask her to make some more copies."

Lester frowned, but simply said, "I got a copier. Won't be color though."

Morehouse waved a hand. "Not important. Can you check the bus station? Signs have a way of walking away from there."

I could tell Lester wondered why Morehouse wasn't making more copies at the police station, but for once he didn't say the first thing on his mind. I said,

"Harry has a copier at the office. We can make a bunch, too."

Morehouse ran a finger through his close-cropped hair. "Thanks."

"You look like crap," Lester said.

"Like I needed a reminder." Morehouse glared. "Most of the volunteers who searched last night are at work or school. I want my sister to know who's looking."

"So, I should call her?"

"You know Karen. Stop by her place, would you, and tell her what you and Lester are doing? And that I asked you to get George involved?"

Lester took an unlit cigar, a constant companion, from a shirt pocket and stuck it between his teeth. "We ain't the only ones looking are we?"

"No, but there's a lot goin' on here today. I need more eyes than we have in cars today. The off-duty guys may look around some." He nodded at me. "Jolie, why don't you check in with me about noon?"

"Okay. I'll ask George to see if the *Ocean Alley Press* will do a story."

Lester and I walked the block to his office. He meets most of his customers in the nearby Burger King, across from the Sandpiper Bar. He says it's because Burger King has better parking.

As we got closer to his building, Lester was his usual blunt self. "I don't mind making copies, but why the hell can't he make them at the station?"

"If I interpreted what he said, he has to be careful about doing lots of stuff right now, because there doesn't seem to be an indication of foul play."

"Yeah, but..." he began.

"Without any suspicious circumstances, if it was another kid Keven's age, the police wouldn't have lots of officers on the street, or make a lot of copies of signs."

Lester bowed to indicate I should precede him up the steps to his office above First Bank. The second floor of the yellow-vinyl-covered frame building held small offices and a couple of apartments. "They'd be searchin' harder if it was a girl."

I thought he was right.

We agreed we'd start with a lot of the small bungalows that served as summer rentals. We were both fairly well known, so people driving by wouldn't think much if we were spotted looking in empty houses. Lester would use the keys to any he had a listing for, and he figured other real estate agents could probably be talked into checking the houses they were selling.

George returned my call while Lester and I studied a map of the two-mile long, twelve-block deep town. "What's up, kid?"

"I'm surprised you haven't heard. Did you know Morehouse's nephew Kevin has been missing for about twenty-four hours, maybe more?"

George said nothing for several seconds. "I was in Ocean Grove much of yesterday. Terry's friend? Can't believe Morehouse didn't call me."

"He told me to. Maybe he figured they'd find him yesterday. Can you get the *Ocean Alley Press* to do an article?"

George worked at the paper before he was fired several years ago for not writing an article about a young woman who faced a mental health crisis – on the public pier. The editor said he might have made the same decision, but it should have been up to him.

Since then, George spent two years as an investigator at an insurance firm, part of a requirement to get a private detective license. He opened his own business investigative agency (he doesn't want us to say detective), and does most of his meetings at Java Jolt coffee house.

"I can tell them he's missing, but they'll take it from there. Can't be sure how they'll pitch it."

Lester butted in. "But they gotta help find him. Who cares what BS they write?"

George heard him. "Hello, Lester."

"Me and Jolie are working up a grid to search empty houses." He turned to me. "I'm thinkin' you do the alphabet streets parallel to the water, and I'll do intersecting streets."

"That's fine, but we'll have to get Terry and his friends, or some other people, to help."

"You have a flyer or something?" George asked.

"Yes," I said. "I think a bunch are up around town."

"Paper probably knows. I'll stop by there, though."

"Morehouse asked me to tell his sister what we're doing, then I'm going to appraise a house on Conch, then I'll meet up with Lester."

Lester started printing copies, so I put a hand over one ear and listened as George said he'd call some local businesses to see if they'd seen Kevin. "Let's meet at Java Jolt about eleven."

"Okay. I'll bring flyers." I hung up and turned to Lester. "Since I know Kevin's mom, I should go there alone. Then I'll call you when I finish the appraisal visit and you can tell me where to hook up."

I've gone to a couple of meetings with Lester. His bluntness could help in some situations, but not with a frantic mother."

I KNEW KAREN FALCON from track meets and a surprise party she planned for Kevin's sixteenth birthday. She's in her mid-forties, roughly ten years older than I am, so we don't socialize a lot. I like her.

The front door of her two-story frame house was open to a glassed storm door. A realtor would call it a modest home, which I knew had only the kitchen, dining, and living rooms on the main floor, and all bedrooms upstairs.

She came to the door as I walked up the steps to her porch. "Jolie. Matthew said you would stop by."

I never call Morehouse by his first name. The twins would probably think it's Sergeant.

Karen's eyes were red and puffy, and her usually carefully styled, blonde hair was pulled into a pony tail. She looked as if she hadn't slept much, if any.

I hugged her as I walked in. "I'll start with vacant houses on B Street, and Lester's starting at Seashore. George is calling businesses. He knows most local owners. Scoobie's got people checking in the ER, in case Kevin comes in."

She gestured to a recliner in the small living room and sat on the couch across from it. "Our other sister, Bella, is flying in from Kansas City this afternoon. I just don't know where else to look!" Her voice cracked and she put a hand over her mouth.

I blew her a kiss as we sat. "We're meeting at Java Jolt at eleven to compare notes, Lester and George and me. I'll walk the boardwalk."

"A bunch of people did that yesterday."

"There could be different staff in the stores or restaurants today. And I'll see if the businesses still closed for the season have phone numbers posted. Kevin is smart. Maybe he's stowed away in one of them."

Karen sniffed and dug into the pocket of her jeans for a tissue. "He worked at the salt water taffy place until the week after school started."

"Did he have a key?"

"I don't think so."

I said nothing while she blew her nose, then asked, "Terry indicated that Kevin seemed upset, and Matthew didn't seem to know why."

She leaned into the couch. "He had gotten a bit...sullen. I chalked it up to a teenager who has a driver's license but isn't allowed to drive his car unless he has a specific destination. One that I know about."

"He and his brother get along well. Does Brian have any ideas?" The twelve-year old spent time with Kevin after school, because Karen worked.

She shook her head. "He's beside himself. Sunday evening Kevin was really agitated. Brian thinks if he told me…"

I interrupted. "I'm sure you tell him nothing is his fault."

"I do. But he won't calm down much until Kevin is home." Her voice cracked, and she steadied it. "I got him to go to school today by telling him he should ask all his friends to keep an eye out for Kevin."

"Did he have any money?"

"He squirrels away what he earns and hides it in the back of his closet, in a boot. The boot's empty, but it couldn't be more than a couple hundred dollars."

My bet would have been more, since he'd worked all summer. "Then he couldn't get too far. Did you check at the bus station?"

"Captain Tortino did that himself. Passenger lists are private unless you get some warrant or something, so he asked the manager to think if Kevin had hung around any buses."

I smiled to myself. About seventeen years ago, a then-Sergeant Tortino had marched me off the boardwalk to Aunt Madge when he saw me smoking a cigarette. It tasted so horrible I wouldn't have kept doing it, so it wasn't hard to promise not to.

"And I take it the manager hadn't seen him?"

"Captain Tortino said the manager let him see he was checking the passenger lists. People can give wrong names if they pay cash, but not that many buses leave Ocean Alley this time of year. No one remembers seeing Kevin. I think they're going to look at some cameras."

Karen frowned. "I can't understand why he didn't take his car."

I shrugged. "Easier to hide himself without it, maybe. And you know he calls it a rust bucket."

She nodded. "It's my old one. He's saving for something a few years newer."

That boot definitely had a good chunk of change.

CHAPTER FOUR

I WAS A REAL ESTATE appraiser in college, and afterwards I worked as a realtor in the my hometown of Lakewood, where my sister Renėe still lives with her husband and two daughters. I picked up the appraiser profession again when I moved to Ocean Alley. In Lakewood I worked largely in commercial real estate, and did not see myself selling cottages or handling beach rental property.

Harry was new in town back then and had recently opened Steele Appraisals, with its office in his home. The Victorian had once belonged to his grandparents, but prior owners had not been kind to it.

He continues to rehab it, and sometimes Aunt Madge or Scoobie help. She sent me to Harry to see about getting a job. I should have figured she had her eye on him.

The work is perfect now. I get half of the appraisal fee and pretty much set my own schedule. Sometimes the twins go to daycare, other times Alicia watches them in between classes at the nearby community college. She loves to babysit, preferably at naptime, so she can study. She's good with them when they're awake, too.

The one-story house on Conch was vacant, which made it easy to measure the rooms and take photos. I found none of the kinds of defects that would bring down the value.

The same couple had owned it for years. They had hoped to sell it before they moved to Florida, but didn't want to lower their price much. Now that they lived far away, I bet they wished they had taken a few thousand less than their initial asking price.

I planned to look for Kevin for a while, meet George and Lester, pick up the kids mid-afternoon, and write up much of the appraisal after the kids went to bed. I could research comparable sales online tonight and at the courthouse tomorrow.

My phone chirped as I started my car. Scoobie. "Hi, hon. You have an early lunch break?"

He spoke so softly I could barely hear him. "Jolie. It looks as if a gash on Sandra Cartwright's head was from a fall, but not after a heart attack. They also found bits of someone else's skin under a couple of her fingernails. As if she scratched them."

I turned off the car. "You mean someone, what? Fought with her?"

"That's not the worst part. If she'd been brought to the hospital she could have lived."

"God, that's horrible. Have the police been at the hospital?"

"Talking to all the nurses, and anyone else she met with the last couple of weeks. For starters."

"She helped Aunt Madge with the campaign because she opposed that big resort hotel. I can't imagine she got in fights with people about it. Or anything else. Do they think someone broke into the house?"

"Her purse is missing. And some of her jewelry."

I frowned. "Sounds like a robbery. Nothing to do with hospital or town politics."

"From what I heard here this morning, she also thought some people on the hospital's board shouldn't be advocating for the project."

"Who?" I asked.

Suspicion oozed from Scoobie's voice. "Why?"

"Remember, Terry said Kevin had talked to Sandra some?"

He stifled a chuckle. "So now you think he could be involved?"

"In her death, of course not. But what did he talk to her about? People say he's been grouchy since he spent a few days in the hospital. Maybe she was, I don't know, helping him or something."

"Gotta get back to work. Had a lull for a couple of minutes, so I thought I'd let you know."

"Did you call Aunt Madge?"

"I'll leave that to you."

AS USUAL, AUNT MADGE was two steps ahead of me. Her friend Gladys on the hospital auxiliary, which Aunt Madge used to head, had called her earlier Tuesday morning.

Distress laced her words. "That wonderful woman. I can't stand that she died alone."

But did she? What if Kevin went there?

"I know. Her purse and some jewelry were missing. Scoobie said, I almost hate to tell you this. Someone else's skin was under a few of her fingernails. Sounds as if the medical examiner might say it was intentional."

Aunt Madge sounded angry. "Whether intentional or accidental, I can't believe the person didn't call 9-1-1. They wouldn't have had to stick around."

"Yesterday you said you were going to call Sergeant Morehouse. Had Sandra told you something?"

She hesitated for a couple of seconds. "She wasn't on the hospital Board of Directors, but she sat in most meetings, and was on the Endowment Committee. The hospital's a nonprofit, of course, and it can't lose money over the long term. Sandra thought the board was…paying too much attention to the bottom line. She sensed some staff cuts were coming because they had fewer patients this past winter."

As someone who's always worked in the private sector, I'm a bottom-line kind of woman. But I'd hate to see staff cuts at the hospital, especially in radiology. Rather than say that, I asked, "Can you really see anyone on that board attacking her in her home if she disagreed with them?"

"Of course not. I…" On her end, someone spoke to Aunt Madge. She conferred with Harry for a moment and came back to me. "Harry reminds me we need to head to the Lions Club lunch for a talk."

"Oh sure. So you are going to keep your schedule?"

"We've decided to keep our appointments, except for the funeral, of course."

"Can you ask if anyone's seen Kevin?"

"I'm asking everyone."

I STOPPED AT THE LIBRARY before going to Java Jolt to meet Lester and George. Head librarian, Daphne, graduated from high school with Scoobie, and I had known her slightly the one year of high school that I lived in Ocean Alley with Aunt Madge. Daphne always knows what's going on around town.

I waited near the customer computers as Daphne finished showing new patrons around the small library. A copy of the *Ocean Alley Press* sat on a table near the reference section. In the BT days, I always read the paper with my morning coffee. Now I'm lucky to glance at the front page.

An interview with hospital CEO Quentin Wharton must have been done before Sandra's cause of death was known. I glanced at the date. Two days ago, before she even died.

Wharton painted a less-than-sanguine picture of hospital finances. I scanned the full article. He talked about low reimbursement rates from Medicare and the need for a younger population of users.

When reporter Tiffany asked him whether he was being an ageist, he said no. It was a matter of balancing the mix of patients with public and private insurance. "I've been a manager in different fields. Quality customer care comes from defining your niche and having the resources to fulfill your goals."

Sounds like he's marketing high-end patio furniture.

Tiffany then asked if he thought the hospital could meet the needs of the community if the resort were built and brought tens of thousands more tourists and a number of new workers to town.

"As you know, I am an advocate for the proposed resort hotel. It would create at least 300 jobs, and would be a strong attraction to potential residential buyers and commercial investors. The hospital will expand to meet the needs. Frankly, we have the capacity to handle more patient volume than we've had recently."

The article continued to another page and I had to laugh when I saw the letters to the editor page next to his continued interview. Sandra Cartwright's letter featured a counter argument. She thought that a dramatic population increase would not only change the character of the town but would tax medical and social services. She also questioned the hospital taking a stand on the resort, "whether through public advocacy or financial support."

I thought the last part did not make total sense. How would the hospital help financially? Then I remembered that a city council vote on the project would be after the election. Even though the winning mayoral or council candidates would not yet be in office, the current council might see the choices as proxy votes for the resort. I supposed the hospital could donate money to the candidates they preferred. Or could they?

Then I spotted Aunt Madge's missive. She mentioned the impact the nine-story, fifty-thousand square foot complex would have on local traffic, and added that its gift shops and spas could drive some longtime local firms out of business. Aunt Madge advocated giving tax breaks to existing businesses or working to bring in more small businesses rather than one large one.

She didn't specifically address the hospital, but echoed Sandra's premise that local investment in a private developer's initiative could be risky. "No one knows when the next big hurricane will hit the coast. How safe will investments be if so many dollars are in one beach bag?"

Finally, Aunt Madge's opponent, a thirty-six year old Ocean Alley native, had his letter. Paul Holley was a class ahead of me the one year I went to high school in Ocean Alley. I hadn't known him. He stayed in Ocean Alley and was a loan officer at the bank and active in the Chamber.

Without raising questions about Aunt Madge's age, he did a good job of excoriating her viewpoint. He saw her views as old-fashioned and the resort as a chance to modernize Ocean Alley. The jobs created would keep residents from leaving when they finished school.

Though I didn't think many of a resort's jobs would support a family, I could see that some people would want more local employment. Holley's campaign had bought a quarter page ad on the page facing the letters to the editor. He and his wife, Meredith, had a teenage son. *They must have started early.*

I went back to Quentin Wharton's interview. He ended by talking about the need to modernize the town. "Right now, downtown Ocean Alley has a kind of faded glory look."

I resented his comment, and pushed aside images of the older brick buildings and cluster of small shops that catered to tourists looking for beachwear and souvenirs. It was all part of Ocean Alley's charm, right?

I would ask George if Tiffany instigated the interview or Wharton called her. It sounded like publicity for the resort. With the city council debating some kind of zoning approval or tax incentive, he probably knew his interview could make a difference.

Daphne walked toward me and I held up a few signs with Kevin's photo.

She nodded her head. "We have a couple on bulletin boards, but if you have extras I'll put them by the circulation desk."

"Morehouse and Kevin's mom would appreciate it." We walked toward her office and I pointed to the paper on the counter. Are you going to throw that out?"

Daphne shook her head. "It's not extra. People keep asking for it because articles and letters talk about the resort. I'm leaving it on the counter for a couple of days."

"Did you know Kevin?"

She narrowed her eyes. "That sounds past tense."

"Gosh, I didn't mean it to."

"I only know him because he's Terry's friend. When your handsome brother-in-law comes in here for his weekly pile of books, Kevin sometimes comes with him."

I smiled. "First you had Scoobie, now Terry." My smile lessened. "Terry said Kevin seemed out of sorts the last couple months, but that appears to be all anyone knows."

"I heard that. I expected more on the news last night."

"Probably seems like a runaway to the media. Morehouse is convinced he left because he's worried or scared about something."

We stopped at the circulation desk and Daphne straightened a stack of brochures that contained library hours. "I'll keep asking people. If I hear anything, should I call Sergeant Morehouse?"

"Yes. If you can't get him, call me or George, and we'll find him."

As I headed to my car, I didn't feel as if I'd accomplished more than leaving the posters. But running the food pantry has taught me that the more you reach out to people, the more invested they become in your mission.

I made it to Java Jolt a couple minutes after eleven. Lester had a city map on a table in front of George, who looked annoyed. "So, Lester," he said, "why do you think he'd be in a vacant house?"

"Kid's smart. He'd hunt for spare keys."

George looked up, and I shrugged in his direction. "He might. Can't go too far without a car."

I sat at their table and waved to Megan, who mimed drinking coffee. I shook my head. "All he had to do was walk a couple miles down the beach and he'd be in Ocean Grove. Lots of houses there, too."

"Crud," Lester said.

"I heard stuff about Sandra at the paper," George said.

Lester pointed his cigar at me. "I liked that dame."

"What did you hear?"

George gave Lester a sideways glance. "You can't repeat this, Lester."

He barked his laugh. "Jolie has the big mouth."

"I do not!"

"Pay attention, you two. Tiffany said she heard a couple senior people at the hospital were angry that Sandra was working on Madge's campaign." George frowned. "Because Madge is working so hard to keep the resort hotel out."

"I read Sandra's letter to the editor. Can't imagine anyone would attack her over whether to build a resort."

Lester shrugged. "Maybe if they had a stake in it."

George and I looked at him.

He pointed his cigar at George. "That Jack Borman guy who wants to build it, he has a reputation of gettin' what he wants. If he's buddied up with that pansy Wharton at the hospital, you can bet he said Wharton should get Sandra to shut up."

I had no retort to that point. I turned to George. "Did Tiffany instigate the interview with Wharton?"

George shook his head. "He called her. She's good, but sometimes she doesn't spot when she's being used."

I shrugged. "It seems what Sandra did on her own time was her business. How likely are some doctors to kill their head nurse?"

"Anyone can off someone if they're mad enough," Lester threw in.

I ignored him. "Which senior people was Tiffany talking about?"

"Working on it," George said, "but I inferred it included Quentin Wharton. He really wants to expand."

The hospital is searching for a new chair of its Board of Directors. In the meantime, no one else on the board wanted to chair it. Wharton is not a voting board member, but for the moment he's acting chair. "Sounds like since he's become interim chair of the hospital's board he's gotten a lot more opinionated."

"If he's acting chair," George said, "he could want to get the permanent appointment. Maybe fewer headaches than running the place day-to-day."

Lester pointed to his map. "I feel bad about the nurse lady, but we gotta find the kid."

CHAPTER FIVE

I HAD WALKED THE town for two hours in the afternoon, and emailed signs to a lot of people. No luck. The twins did enjoy the long stroll.

All the open boardwalk stores would have been searched, but if Kevin wanted to hide in a seasonal business that wasn't open yet, he could have gone in last night, or earlier today.

I glanced at my watch. I had about forty-five minutes before Scoobie would be home from his Tuesday evening Alcoholics Anonymous meeting, which he always goes to with George. He would wonder why I'd asked Aunt Madge to drink a cup of tea in our house while Terry made signs at the library and the twins slept.

Aunt Madge thought I went to the grocery store. I had milk and a box of mac and cheese already in the car. They were my alibi in case Scoobie didn't like the idea of me poking around dark boardwalk stores – which I knew he wouldn't.

I parked on Ferry Street and hustled up the wooden staircase that led from the street to the boardwalk. With the forty-five-degree temps and hint of rain to come, the boardwalk was deserted. I glanced at the ocean. When it's dark-colored at night, the whitecaps look like frosting on chocolate cake.

My primary target was the salt water taffy store, where Kevin had worked part-time until Labor Day. Store owner Frank Fitzpatrick had surely checked his store, as Morehouse had asked all owners of closed stores to do. But would Kevin have a key?

I peered through the plate glass window, taking in the huge, metal machine that swirled taffy, much to tourists' delight. Shelves behind the counter held a couple dozen boxes of taffy. A brightly colored sign on the wall said, "Best Taffy on the Jersey Shore."

Behind the counter was a closed door that led to a storage room. Maybe the store's back door, on the alley, would have a window. As I turned, a brief flicker of light drew my eyes to the bottom of the interior door. Was someone using a flashlight or candle?

I almost ran to the alley. The salt water taffy place was three stores down from the boardwalk steps. I saw no flicker of light in the rear door's window, but I felt certain I didn't imagine it.

If Kevin were inside, he likely would not respond to my knock. I tried anyway. No response. I decided to act as I did when a twin had a meltdown – wait it out.

The three concrete steps from the alley to the door were hard and cold. I pulled my fleece hoodie over my head and zipped it up. I sat on the bottom step, sideways, back against one of the posts that supported the railing. I wanted Kevin to see my face.

Who are you kidding? He's not going to be here.

I looked up and down the narrow, asphalt-paved alley. Waves rushing the sand barely made a sound behind the store. Quiet reigned and I saw no one else.

As I was about to get off my cold backside and head home, a deadbolt turned behind me. I glanced toward the door.

A whispered voice said, "Jolie?"

"Hi, Kevin. Can I come in?"

"Yeah. But don't let anyone see me."

I stood, climbed two steps, and let myself into the dark back room of Ocean Alley Salt Water Taffy.

Kevin had backed up, but remained stooped over. "Close the door fast!"

I complied. "Thanks for letting me in."

"Can you please sit on the floor?"

"Sure." As my eyes adjusted to the dim light, I took in boxes of supplies, counter-height surfaces, and Kevin's much-thinner face and tired eyes. I also detected the distinctive smell of teenage-boy-in-need-of-a-shower.

"Do you have any food? Everything in here is sweet."

I took a plastic bag of broken animal crackers from my pocket and passed it to him. "Better than taffy. I'd be happy to take you somewhere to eat."

He shook his head as he accepted the crackers. "No one would look for me here."

I smiled. "Present company excluded?"

He popped a cracker in his mouth. "Oh, right."

"What's up, Kevin? You don't need me to tell you everyone is sick with worry about you."

He leaned against a counter and closed his eyes. "I know, and I'm sorry. I don't want anyone else to get hurt."

"Can you start at the beginning for me?"

He stared at me as he chewed, frowning and uncertain.

"You can't stay in here forever. You have to trust someone."

That got me a quick smile. "Terry says you know how to figure out stuff."

"I try. I can also find a way to keep you safe." I wanted to say after we called his mom and Morehouse, but I left that out for the moment.

He gave the deepest sigh I'd ever heard from a kid. "Okay, so you remember when I had my appendix out, right?"

I nodded. "And you had an infection, so you were in there for a few days."

"Yeah. Plus I waited too long to tell Mom I felt bad, so it was pretty swollen or something."

I tried to look encouraging.

"So, when I was still sort of asleep – it was freezing in there – I thought I heard people talking about some money for the hospital, and a nurse who didn't want them to have it."

He fished the last animal cracker out of the bag. "I wanted to say I'd take the money, but I couldn't get my mouth to move."

I smiled. "You could have heard a conversation, or part of one. Sometimes you're in deeper sleep than other times."

"I think it was after they operated." He shrugged. "After you wake up, you're kind of in a fog."

"You were probably in the recovery room," I said.

"Yeah, that's it. I asked the nurse why my side hurt, and it sure did. Then someone, another man, said 'it's your job to convince her.' I think the men were standing by the wall. Maybe…" His expression brightened. "A tour. Somebody said that." He frowned. "And then something about watching somebody's back."

I couldn't figure out why what he heard frightened him, but I didn't want to rush Kevin. "Bottom line, something about all this seemed wrong?"

He nodded and shrugged at the same time. "Mostly made me wonder. When I woke up more I talked to the nurse helping me. I asked her what about convincing a nurse to take care of the something?"

I nodded, still trying to look encouraging.

"She didn't get it. She just said she was taking care of me. And I think that's when the two men left. Do you have any other food?"

"No, but we can stop at McDonald's on the way back to your house."

His head shake was emphatic. "I think the nurse, Ms. Cartwright, was killed because I didn't tell anyone what I heard."

Younger kids sometimes think all events around them relate to them. But Kevin was sixteen. "You'll have to help me see that link."

"Okay, so Terry's Aunt Madge knows her. Ms. Cartwright."

"Yes. For a long time."

"I could tell that. I saw them working together at that last food pantry fundraiser. The one where Scoobie said he was pirate-in-chief."

I rolled my eyes. "I'd forgotten she helped Aunt Madge round up people for the bake sale at our second Talk Like a Pirate Day event."

"Right. So, I looked her up, and went to her house."

"Sandra Cartwright's house? You went there."

"Couple of weeks ago. I'd seen those articles in the paper about the new hotel, and how Aunt Madge was against it because it would cost the city a lot of money, or something. And then this guy was interviewed, I think the guy who wants to build it. He said he would give a lot of money to the hospital if the hotel got built."

"And it reminded you of the conversation you heard in the recovery room?"

"Yep. I asked Mom about the new hotel but, you know, she's always busy."

I nodded. "Hard to be a single parent."

"So, anyway, I went to Ms. Cartwright's house, maybe ten days ago, and asked her if she thought someone was out to get a nurse. That's the only part that really bothered me."

"And what did Sandra say?"

"Well, first off, she believed me. She really listened. She said there were 'honest differences' between people, the ones who wanted the hotel and the ones who didn't." He leaned over to tie a shoestring that looked pretty tight to me.

I studied his bowed head. "Sandra didn't want it built."

"She said that. And she kind of laughed and said she was probably the nurse the people hoped would be quieter."

I waited for him to say more, and when he didn't, I said, "I'm not getting something, Kevin. What does this have to do with you leaving home? Why are you so frightened?"

His eyes filled. "After I saw her letter to the editor, you know, day before yesterday, I went to her house. And, and…" He put his head on his knees and sobbed.

I scooted next to him and put one hand on his shoulder. "Kevin, are you saying that you saw her? After Sandra died?"

His shoulders simply shook, and two tears fell to the floor.

I grabbed my purse and drew out some McDonald's napkins from the twins' last round of Happy Meals. "Here, Kevin. Sit up and blow your nose. We'll try to make it better for you."

His sobs slowed and he took the napkins, but he didn't take his head off his knees. "You don't get it. The man saw me at her door. He was on the side of her house, and he saw me and ran."

I kept my tone gentle. "Maybe you can help your uncle, uh, figure out who that was."

He lifted his head. "You still don't get it! I knew something was wrong when she didn't answer. I tried her door. It was unlocked, so I went in, and she was…just there. On the floor." The tears began again, with even louder sobs.

"I'm so sorry, Kevin. You shouldn't have had to see that."

He raised his head. "She shouldn't be dead!" His head went to his knees again.

"Of course not." My thoughts jumbled together. He'd had the shock of finding her, probably with blood near the body. Plus, he was afraid the man he saw was her killer and would be after him.

"Kevin, we need to call your uncle. He can figure out what to do."

He sat up and wiped a hand across both eyes. "But if I go home, they might come after Mom and Brian. I need to stay away."

I spoke with all the conviction I could muster. "Sergeant Morehouse will know how to keep all of you safe. We can go to the station and you can describe the man you saw. They'll catch him."

He shook his head.

I spoke firmly. "You'll be able to think better after you have a good meal. And you *must* let your mom know you're okay. She's worried sick."

"I don't know."

No way I could make him do anything, and if I called the police to safely transport him, Kevin could be gone before anyone got here. I tried another tactic. "Think about it. If I found you, someone else might. We need to get you to a safe place."

"Why did you look here?"

"Didn't take a lot of deep thought. You worked here, I thought you might have a key."

He sighed. "Mister Fitzpatrick came in yesterday. I piled boxes and hid in the back of the storage closet. He was muttering about being late for bowling and didn't look hard."

I smiled. "It's cold on this floor. How about if I drive you home?"

"I'll go to the police station. I don't want anyone looking for me at home." He scrambled to his feet and reached a hand to help me up.

I shivered. "Terry found your coat. You must be cold."

"Yeah. I was walking around and realized I had blood on my sleeve." He sniffed. "Ms. Cartwright's blood, from when I pressed her neck for a pulse. Anyway, I took off the coat."

I decided not to ask him if he found a pulse. Surely if he had he would have called 9-1-1. "Come on. The station is just five blocks away. You have the key to lock up?"

He nodded and gestured that I should walk out ahead of him. "He keeps one hidden, taped to the top outside step. Not a good hiding place."

I stood at the bottom of the steps as he locked the door. Kevin's fears had me spooked, and I glanced up and down the now dark alley.

"My car's on the street, just a couple doors down."

He came down the steps and turned to follow me. We walked briskly. I popped the locks and made for my door, which was on the sidewalk side. Kevin had almost reached the front passenger door when bright car lights came on about twenty yards from us.

As Kevin shielded his eyes, the car pulled out and sped toward him. Kevin took a few quick steps, but he wasn't going to be able to get to my side of the car fast enough.

I stared at the car's front bumper, all I could make out in the bright headlights. No dents, but a long scratch almost looked as if someone had run a key along it.

Kevin jumped up and rolled across the hood of my car, landing on the sidewalk next to my front tire.

The car never slowed. Its tires squealed and it turned left onto B Street without slowing.

I bent over, "Kevin, are you…"

"Leave me alone!" He jumped up, turned toward the ocean, and ducked under the raised boardwalk. In three seconds he had vanished.

CHAPTER SIX

HELL HATH NO FURY like a tired toddler or a distraught police sergeant.

I fumed as I responded to his outburst. "I told you, we were coming to the station. If I'd called for you to send a car he would've left."

Morehouse's yell could probably be heard at the station entrance. "Same difference! Did you even get a look at the damn car?"

I shook my head. "The headlights were right in my eyes. Kind of a mid-size car. Maybe a narrow scratch on the bumper."

"That's no damn help!"

Sergeant Dana Johnson spoke many decibels below her colleague. "So, Jolie, you say he ran under the boardwalk. Toward the kiddie rides or away from them?"

"North, away from the rides. Toward Ocean Grove." My phone chirped and I glanced at it. "It's Scoobie. I have to answer."

As I said hello, Sergeant Morehouse stomped out of his office and into the bullpen, spewing instructions. Dana winked at me and followed him. I hoped she could calm him down some. What if he called Karen when he was full of vitriol?

Scoobie sounded relieved. "When Aunt Madge said she expected you back before I got here, I was worried."

"I'm good. When I was coming back from the store I had a wild idea. I went to the back door of the salt water taffy place."

Scoobie's silence said a lot.

"Anyway, Kevin was there, and…"

"That's great, did you call Terry? He's with some of the other…"

"It was good, but Kevin didn't stick around." I relayed what had happened without mentioning that a vehicle tried to mash Kevin into my car.

"That's nuts. He just ran away from you?"

I swallowed. "He had some encouragement."

A tone I recognized as one of suspicion crept into Scoobie's voice. "Encouragement how?"

"I'm not sure if it was as deliberate as it seemed, but a car kind of…came at him. Kevin rolled over my hood, landed on the sidewalk, and took off."

A protracted silence followed. "Scoobie?"

"When are you coming home, Jolie?"

"Soon, I think. I came to the station to tell them. Dana and Sergeant Morehouse are getting some folks organized to try to track Kevin. Toward Ocean Grove, I think."

Scoobie sighed. "I'll call Terry. We'll talk when you get home."

I didn't want to feel like a chastised kid, but part of me knew I'd been reckless.

SCOOBIE SAID HE HAD checked on the kids just before I got home. He sat on the couch, feet on the coffee table with that day's *Ocean Alley Press* on his lap. At least I'd remembered to bring in the bag with milk and mac 'n cheese that I'd put in the car to mask my intent.

"Let me stick the milk in the fridge." I did that, poured myself a glass of water, and returned to the living room.

Scoobie patted the spot next to him on the couch and put the paper aside. "You really expect me to believe going to the taffy place was a last-minute thought?"

I shrugged, and kept from saying he could believe what he wanted to. "I was heading back from Mr. Markle's store, on B Street, thinking about Kevin. When it crossed Ferry Street, — you know, it goes near the back of the salt water taffy store — I suddenly had this strong feeling that since Kevin worked there last summer, he could have a key."

"Jolie, what if that car had hit you? After I put the kids to bed I would've had to call the funeral home."

"Aunt Madge probably would have done it for you." My attempt at humor fell flat.

"Joke all you want. Doesn't make it funny."

"I don't think any of it was. Every time I passed a car on the way home, I wondered if it was that car. There's no way to know."

I relayed what Kevin had said. "Do you think someone tried to convince Sandra of something and killed her when they couldn't?"

"You're missing the point. If Kevin were to call us for a ride home, that's one thing. But to actively look for him now is crazy."

The thoroughly read copy of *A Child's Garden of Verses* rested under the coffee table and I reached for it. "I agree that it's crazy now that we know what he saw and that someone may not want him going to the police. But I didn't know any of that."

"And I'm your husband not the detention hall proctor. But you've got to promise me to butt out one-hundred percent. A killer knows you found Kevin once. They might follow you and the kids to see if you're going to pick him up somewhere."

The house phone rang and I looked at caller ID. "Aunt Madge."

Scoobie stood. "I'm going to check upstairs to make sure Lance stayed in his bed."

"Hi, Aunt Madge."

"Why on earth didn't you take Sergeant Morehouse or Dana with you?"

I thought for a second that we were both a bit sexist because we usually called Morehouse by his title, and his younger colleague by her first name. I gave a shortened version of events. Before she could ask a question, I did. "Have you heard about anyone else who was mad at Sandra?"

Two beats of silence. "I'm thinking a lot about Sandra, but my focus is on you, young lady."

Uh-oh. She called me young lady. "I'm not the one who rolled on the sidewalk. I wish I'd been fast enough to tackle Kevin."

"In your dreams. Where is Terry?" Aunt Madge asked.

"Not here, but it's…" I looked at my watch, "almost nine. He should be home soon."

Her tone was clipped. "You and I need to make a deal. If I'm watching the twins, I need to know where you're going. If the people driving that car had pulled you into it, we wouldn't have had a clue where to send the police to look for you."

I spoke meekly. "I hear you." Then I added, "Why don't you call a few of your friends in Ocean Grove? Our boardwalk doesn't stretch all the way there, but much of the way. Maybe he headed that way and someone will see him."

"I'll call one of the B&B owners up there."

A car door banged at our curb. "I think Terry just got dropped off."

"Call me tomorrow." She hung up.

Terry almost threw himself into the living room. "You found him and then you lost him?"

"Not exactly." I relayed only the tail end of the story, not saying what Kevin had heard at the hospital, just that he thought Sandra's murderer had seen him. And might think Kevin could identify the killer.

Terry's brow furrowed as he sank into the rocker. "So why run? He didn't do anything wrong."

"He doesn't want whoever may be after him to find him when he's with his mom or brother."

Scoobie had padded softly down the steps so Terry and I didn't notice him until he walked into the living room. "I told Jolie we need to be careful that someone doesn't think she's a link to Kevin's hiding place." He sat next to me.

Terry pounded a fist on the rocker's arm. "We have to find him!"

"Not tonight," Scoobie said.

Terry looked at me and I held his gaze. "Sergeant Morehouse is organizing people to search. Unless you have a specific place to suggest, the best thing we can all do is get some sleep so we can look tomorrow."

Scoobie raised one eyebrow. "We?"

I spoke quickly. "As part of whatever search group the police are organizing."

Terry's voice rose. "But now we know he's still in town. He might come out if I'm the one walking around."

I tilted my head toward the twins' baby monitor. "And you'd be walking the streets by yourself…"

"Or with Scoobie," Terry said.

Scoobie shook his head. "I have to be at work at seven."

Terry's face reddened. "So, we just go to bed and Kevin could be hiding in a trash barrel or something?"

GIVEN TERRY'S LEVEL OF FRUSTRATION, I shouldn't have been surprised that his bed was empty Wednesday morning. Still, he'd never disobeyed us about something this important. I wasn't sure how to divide my mix of worry and anger.

Leah's voice came down the hall. "Mommy? I think I have my shoes on backwards."

I turned and started for where she stood, in the hall outside the twin's bedroom. "On the wrong feet?"

Lance's voice came from their shared bedroom. "Yeah, Leah. Not backwards."

I smiled as I reached Leah. "Come on, let's get them on the other feet."

I sat in the bedroom rocker and pulled her onto my lap. Her hair still smelled of last night's douse of baby shampoo. I sniffed.

"Here, watch how I tie it. Some day you can tie your own shoes."

Leah watched intently, but Lance distracted her as he threw a foam ball toward the three-foot tall basketball hoop. He missed.

"Better luck next time, brother."

I started to laugh, and Lance glared at me. "I'm laughing because you're both silly."

Leah pointed to the wallpaper, with its mix of Sesame Street characters. "Elmo's silly."

"Cookie Monster's sillier," Lance added.

Scoobie's voice carried down the hall. "Come on, Terry. It's six-forty and…"

He must have reached Terry's door and realized the bed had not been slept in.

"Jolie?"

I looked toward the door of the kids' bedroom. "In here. And I just saw the empty bed half-a-minute ago."

Scoobie came to the doorway. "Morning kidlets." He looked at me. "You hear him leave?"

I shook my head and focused on tying Leah's second sneaker.

"It'll be an unexcused absence. All he needs is detention. Track coach will throw…" he scowled at my laugh as I sat Leah on the floor.

"Gee, hon, we've never known anyone in detention."

Lance tossed his foam ball into the toy box. "My points! What's de-ten-shun?"

"It means you stay after school," I said.

"Do you get more pineapple juice?" Leah asked.

I ignored the question. "Come on you two. I want us to leave for daycare the same time Daddy leaves for work. We can stop at Arnie's Diner for pancakes."

Scoobie and I each carried a twin to the Odyssey. He was in his car and out of the driveway before I had them both strapped into their carriers. I love having a van big enough for Terry's friends, twin gear, and whatever else, but sometimes I feel like I'm about to pilot a boat.

As I settled behind the steering wheel, Lance asked, "Is Daddy mad at Terry?"

"He wishes Terry had told us what time he'll be home."

"Track practice starts at three. No one can be late," Leah recited.

Other than the lack of sleep, there are many wonderful things about being a mom to twins. The best is I get a bunch of belly laughs every day.

AFTER WE HAD PANCAKES and I dropped off the twins, I headed for Mr. Markle's In-Town Grocery. He would know Kevin was missing, and he probably also knew grocers in Ocean Grove who could keep watch for him. I could email the signs Morehouse made.

I entered the small store and gazed toward the produce section. Mr. Markle is often in that part of the store keeping the fruit and vegetables orderly. The green linoleum floors are old and the aisles narrow, but the store is always clean. Plus, he'll order anything he doesn't regularly stock. He also gives the food pantry big discounts if we suddenly need milk or PB&J.

I located him near the bananas and explained finding and losing, Keven, and the direction he headed.

He reached for an over-ripe kiwi and stuck it in the waist pocket of his huge white apron. "How do you know Kevin went that far?"

"I don't. But it could make sense."

He smiled, but the motion didn't reach his eyes. "Terry thought so, too. I've already called my friend Bob at Ocean Grove Produce. Terry texted him a copy of the sign with Kevin's picture."

I blew out a breath as we turned to walk toward the cash register together. "He, uh, got up really early today."

"I'll say. He met me by the back door when I was taking the milk delivery. Terry said Kevin running away had something to do with Sandra's murder?"

I hadn't planned to mention that. "It might. Sort of."

"But he isn't a suspect, is he?"

"No, no, of course not."

We stopped at the end of an aisle, near the exit. I expelled a breath. "I just wish I knew where else to look for him."

"Not likely that you personally would find him again. Why don't you focus on whatever it is he's afraid of? Terry seemed unsure of all the details."

"Good idea." As Mr. Markle turned his attention to the baskets of strawberries, I asked, "Are you okay? You seem tired or something."

He turned back to me. "Did you know I've had an offer to sell the store to the resort developers?"

I swallowed. "I didn't. A good offer?"

"Since I own the land as well as the building, it was hefty."

Why is he telling me this? "You giving it some serious thought?"

"I might. Probably would think more about it if the guy making the offer wasn't such a jerk. You met Jack Borman?"

I thought for a moment. "He's the lead developer, isn't he?"

"Yes. Believes his resort will be God's gift to Ocean Alley. Or he is."

I debated giving him my honest impression about selling, and decided he'd earned it. "I was in commercial real estate before I moved to Ocean Alley. Much as I hope you won't sell, property values are fickle. If it's a good offer, you should really think about it."

"And what would I do with my time?"

That struck me as an odd question. If I had a big sum, I could think of one-hundred things to do. Starting with hiring a full-time housekeeper and cook so I could spend non-work time with Scoobie and the kids. Maybe get my nails done now and then. "No plans to buy a cabin cruiser?"

He snorted. "No one to cruise with. I think I'd rather work."

I realized he had come to our wedding solo. "Is there a Mrs. Markle?"

"Was."

I flushed. "I'm sorry."

He concentrated on a batch of rhubarb. "Cancer, a few years before you came to town."

"You'll, uh, have to come over for Sunday dinner, sometime."

"Scoobie cooking?"

CHAPTER SEVEN

MR. MARKLE'S IDEA OF FOCUSING ON the possible core of Kevin's fear was a good one. I headed to Ocean Alley Hospital.

Along the way I considered that the loss of the In-Town Grocery store would really change the character of downtown Ocean Alley. A lot of older, and poorer, people shopped there because the bus went by it. They had to take a cab to the Wal-Mart outside of town.

More than that, business people ducked into the store all the time to get snacks or cleaning supplies for their offices. Tourists frequented it all summer, to get supplies for their weekend or weekly rentals.

I stuck an earbud in my ear and called George. "Did you know the resort developer has made an offer to buy the In-Town Grocery?"

"Can't say I'm surprised. He's known for presenting a town with plans for a development, getting some tax benefits or whatever, and then going for more. Probably trying to do as much of a land grab as he can."

I entered the hospital parking lot. "You sound like you know a lot about him."

"Just that he likes to get what he wants. Why are you asking?"

"Talking to Mr. Markle, it made it seem more real. Ocean Alley could turn into a mostly tourist town, without the kinds of connections we have now."

"You've been listening to your aunt. Gotta run to an appointment."

I walked slowly into the main entrance. Scoobie is never pleased when I roam the hospital halls. Unless we're there for something fun, from his point of view, like Lamaze classes. He certainly doesn't tell me where to go any more than I tell him. He just doesn't like the looks he gets in the cafeteria when I've been poking around.

I headed for the executive suite on third floor. The carpet's deep pile sets off the suite for the big shots from the rest of the hospital. That and the hushed environment always make me feel like a kid headed to the principal's office.

CEO Quentin Wharton has to at least pretend to be glad to see me, because Scoobie works here and I once solved the murder of a hospital employee. I entered his outer office, noting the closed door to his inner sanctum.

Quentin's admin assistant, who always looked as if she'd just stepped from a make-up artist's chair, greeted me with a wary look.

I gave her my most dazzling smile. "Hi, Clarissa. I wanted to talk to Quentin about the Cinco de Mayo fundraiser. Just for a minute."

"He's about to leave for a meeting with the senior nursing staff, but I'll see." She picked up her phone.

I glanced at the woman, Marleen, who sat at the opposite desk. "So sad about Sandra Cartwright."

She nodded. "I was unit clerk on pediatrics when she was the charge nurse. She was easy-going with staff and patients."

Clarissa hung up her phone. "He can give you five minutes, Jolie. If you need more you can schedule an appointment as you leave."

"Thanks." I walked the few steps to the series of hospital photos on a wall. They traced its growth from a one-story clinic to its current three wings and three stories. A framed piece of word art ended the display. It said, "Still growing and serving Ocean Alley."

Wharton opened the door to his office. I turned toward him, and he gestured that I should enter. "Busy week for you, I imagine."

I made my nod a solemn one. "Not as busy as most of yours, I'm sure." I took a proffered chair across from his desk as he sat behind it. "We appreciate that the hospital will have a presence at the festival."

"Happy to be there. I hope the fundraiser attracts a crowd that we usually only see in the emergency room. We have some information about how to get a primary care physician. Should cut down on ER use." He glanced at a message on his phone.

"In English and Spanish?"

He nodded. "Plus a small coloring book that shows kids visiting a doctor for check-ups. We'll have a donation jar, but won't make it a requirement to get the book."

"What a great idea! The Lions are doing a bean bag toss. That attracts the kids. We'll try to put it next to your space."

His smile was thin. "You didn't just stop by to discuss Harvest for All."

"Mostly. I also wanted to say I'm sorry about Sandra. She and Aunt Madge have been friends for years."

Wharton checked his phone again. "I can't imagine she knew anyone who would kill her. Or her being fooled into letting in a stranger."

"I've heard a couple people speculate that her death had something to do with her opposition to the resort."

He spread his hands and then rested them on his desk. "Ridiculous! People talk about that resort as if it's a brothel or a… a junk yard. The developer could take that project to a lot of towns and he chose Ocean Alley."

His face reddened. "And look who's working on it. The current mayor, half the Chamber of Commerce, heck, some of our own board. For which, as you know, I serve as interim chair while the search committee finds a new one. Hardly a gang of murderers."

The prior board chair, Jason Logan, was a pompous man, who always seemed to imply that people should bow in his presence. Scoobie said any employees who dealt with him were glad that he left.

I'd always thought of Quentin Wharton as Logan's lap dog. Today he definitely had a more vigorous demeanor. Maybe being interim board chair gave him a chance to deal with the board and a mix of town and medical leaders as an equal. I bet he relished the role.

I smiled. "If the resort brings in the volume of new employees and tourists people say it will, it should increase your patient load."

He stood. "We'll manage or expand. You might let your aunt know that."

I rose. "She tries to stay on top of things. Did you hear that Sergeant Morehouse's nephew has been missing a couple of days?"

His raised eyebrows and wide eyes seemed an exaggerated look of surprise.

"I'm pulling together all the input for our long-range plan. First draft is due to the board Thursday. I've been practically living in this building."

And not talking to anyone? "It seems he may have been one of the last people to see Sandra alive."

We moved toward the door. "Good Lord. He's not a suspect is he?"

"I don't think so."

"Perhaps it's better if Kevin doesn't make himself too visible until the killer is arrested."

Since I hadn't said his name, I figured Quentin Wharton not only knew Kevin was missing, but maybe what had scared him.

As we reached the door, I turned to face him. "Did Sandra talk to you about any of her conversations with Kevin? I think she knew something was worrying him."

He stood next to me frowning. "Do you know what it was?"

"Kevin had an emergency appendectomy not too long ago. In the recovery room, he thought he heard a couple of people talking about a nurse who didn't agree with something, and something about watching her back."

Wharton's frown lifted. "People say and do all kinds of things as they wake up. I'm told that after a hernia repair, I asked the recovery room nurse to take the stapler off the wall."

"And did she?"

He looked at his phone again. "I have to get going. Just keep in mind that he probably had a dream, or put together unrelated things he heard."

He opened the door for me, and I walked into the reception area. A man with thinning hair studied the photos of the hospital. He half-turned quickly toward Wharton then turned back to the picture.

"Hey, Peter," Wharton said. "Don't think I have you on my schedule."

"Just leaving those new insurance estimates."

I paid no attention to the man and continued into the executive suite hallway.

I WASN'T SURE HOW to proceed. I did need to find Terry. Before Scoobie left for work we agreed that I would stop by school to make sure Terry had shown up for class.

Anger mixed with understanding when I thought about him leaving the house before we rose this morning. I got that he wanted to search for his friend, but felt irritated that he hadn't left a note. I didn't worry that he had imitated his friend and taken off.

As I drove toward the high school, I surveyed the quiet streets. On Saturday, streets would teem with adults and kids heading for the Harvest for All Cinco de Mayo celebration on the boardwalk.

Ocean Alley's mix of bungalows and small apartment buildings, nearly all of frame construction, gives the town its allure. If the resort was built, it wouldn't mean all of the smaller residences and apartments would vanish immediately. However, the resort would create an incentive for people to sell to developers who wanted to build larger complexes. Our children would grow up in a very different Ocean Alley.

I pulled into visitor parking at the high school at nine o'clock. School security protocols meant the front door was locked, with a security guard sitting just inside. I pressed my nose to the glass in the door, and waved at the older woman. I thought her name was Jeanine and was glad that she wore a name badge that confirmed it. She let me in.

"Hi, Jeanine. I wanted to check on something for the Harvest for All fundraiser."

White lie. White lie.

She nodded. "I saw a sign that said the Student Council was looking for volunteers for some kind of game they're running." She waved me toward the office.

I entered the office and signed the visitor log. A quick glance around the space that held multiple support staff desks told me they were busy tallying attendance and deciding which absences merited a call to parents. I had done this when I volunteered in the office last year when a flu outbreak decimated the staff.

I wanted to know if Terry had come to school. I wasn't sure what I would do if he hadn't.

A woman's voice called from across the room. "Jolie, come on over." Barbara Burns has worked at the high school for more than twenty years and, as she says, knows every trick in the book.

I nodded at a couple other people as I made my way to her. "Hi Barbara. I won't lie, Terry left early to hunt for Kevin. I want to make sure he showed up for class."

She turned to her computer and tapped a few keys. "I don't understand any of this. Kevin, he's a good boy."

I didn't want to get into any explanations, so I said simply, "He is."

She peered at the screen. "Terry was in homeroom. Teachers note absences in the system for each class. Do you want me to check beyond homeroom?"

I did, but said no. "Thanks. Now if I can slip out quietly Terry will never know I checked up on him. It's a tough time for him."

Barbara nodded. "You still holding the fundraiser?"

"I'm on my way to the Purple Cow now. They ordered a bunch of Cinco de Mayo flags for us to hang along the boardwalk rails."

After extracting the promise that Barbara would attend for a while on Saturday, I headed for the exit. I had almost reached it when a familiar voice came down the hall. "Yo, Jolie."

Scoobie has called to me that way since we were in high school. Terry rarely does, but he probably figured it would soften me up. I turned toward the sound of his voice and he loped toward me, his backpack slung over one shoulder.

He stopped only a foot from me and bent over to kiss my cheek. "I should have left a note."

I patted his elbow as he pulled back. "Yes, you should have. How'd you get to school?"

"A lot of people are looking."

"Any luck?"

He shook his head. "I've got permission from one of the counselors for a bunch of us to head to the boardwalk during lunch. You can mostly see when someone is under there, but there are spots where someone could hide."

I looked at his shoes. He wore what Lance called Terry's crummy shoes. He had heard Terry use the term once and adopted it, the little mimic.

"I went over to the hospital. Nada."

Terry frowned. "That's the last place he'd go."

"Voluntarily." I regretted the word as soon as I said it. "I don't really think anything bad would happen to him. Scoobie can keep an eye out for him."

A bell sounded, and Terry pointed down the hall. "Math class."

I watched him half jog away. We were spinning our wheels. Kevin would only be found when he felt safe enough to come out of hiding.

CHAPTER EIGHT

SCOOBIE'S SLOW PACE UP THE house steps told me either he was carrying something heavy or didn't feel good. I opened the door for him. "What's up?"

"Let me make a cocktail and I'll tell you."

I smiled. His cocktails consisted of seltzer water and cranberry juice. "Okay. Kids haven't stirred so we have a few minutes to ourselves."

He wiggled his eyebrows at me as he walked toward the kitchen.

I raised the front window to let in the spring air, then sat on the couch.

When Scoobie entered with his icy drink he bore a grim expression.

"I got an official reprimand at work today."

I sat up straighter. "What? What could you possibly have done?"

He shook his finger at me, but smiled. "I believe the appropriate response would be how could they have made such a mistake?"

I flushed. "Of course. Tell me about it."

He pulled a folded piece of paper from the pocket of his scrubs and handed it to me. "It says they've had two patient complaints about rudeness."

I read the reprimand, which did indeed say that. "I can't imagine you being rude."

"When my boss sat me down to talk about it, he was surprised, too. The first thing Sam tells anyone who comes to work in radiology is not to let anything a patient does get to us. You know I deflect rudeness with humor. Besides, I cut everybody a lot of slack. When people are hurting, sometimes they say things they don't mean."

"I know you don't have a union, but isn't there some process for discussion before you get a letter like this?"

"That's the way it's supposed to work. It almost feels as if I've been singled out."

I swallowed. "Do you think it has anything to do with Aunt Madge's campaign?"

"Or perhaps my wife's conversations with the hospital CEO?"

"I hardly said anything when I talked to him!" I didn't want to throw Aunt Madge under the bus, but she is a tough bird. "Um. Maybe it was her most recent letter to the editor."

"Could be. People know my connection to Aunt Madge. Bottom line, I think this is supposed to tell us to back off."

I stared at him. "We can't risk your job, but it's hard to know what to back off of. Asking questions about Sandra's murder? Figuring out what Kevin heard after his surgery?"

Scoobie nodded slowly. "And we certainly can't tell Aunt Madge to tone it down."

"Harry kind of tries. Or at least, he diverts the conversation when she goes over the same issues." It felt like a lame comment as soon as I said it.

"We can find some kind of employment lawyer to formally ask questions if some powers that be try anything else. But if we had to go that route, I would probably have to look for another job. We might have to leave Ocean Alley."

I'VE RELOCATED BEFORE. BUT I had no intention of letting someone at the hospital force us out of Ocean Alley. I glanced at the clock on Aunt Madge's stove. I had let the dogs out as soon as I got to the Cozy Corner, but if I didn't get the loaves of bread in the oven in ten minutes they would not be ready for afternoon tea.

I punched the rising dough on one of the two loaves. It felt good to have something to take out my anger on. Once Sandra's killer was caught, it would become clear whether her death was the result of a burglar who surprised her or someone angry with her opposition to the resort. Or something else.

I often think by writing a list of questions or to-do items, but I had flour on my fingers. What did I need to know?

Sandra didn't work the day of her death. Who did she talk to? And how would I figure that out? We knew she had a head injury, but had she fallen and hit her head during an argument, or did someone strike her?

I probably wouldn't be able to poke around about the medical examiner's report – if it had even been issued. Knowing he would work as an investigator, George had kept up his contacts all over town. He should be able to find out.

Quentin Wharton clearly knew Kevin was missing. His feigned lack of knowledge about him bothered me. I couldn't seek him out again, and if he sat at the hospital's booth at the Cinco de Mayo Festival, I might not get a chance to broach any topic, let alone a sensitive one.

Deciding to put George to work gave me a sense of accomplishment. I stuck the loaves in the oven and turned to making tea.

WHEN THE GUESTS WERE EATING, I called George. "I want to know more about Sandra's cause of death and whether Quentin Wharton knows anything about it."

"Gee, Jolie, so good to hear from you. Beautiful day, isn't it?"

I stuck my tongue out at the phone. "Sorry. Can you do some digging? I may have worn out my welcome at the hospital for a while."

He laughed. "Imagine that. What do you want to know?"

I outlined my thoughts.

George said nothing for several seconds, then spoke slowly. "I can probably find out more about her cause of death. The paper might have received a summary of the ME's report."

81

Frustration crept into my tone. "But even if we know how, we don't know why. She wrote that negative letter to the editor, about the resort. People listen to her. Maybe someone felt threatened."

"The thing is, Jolie, the people who will decide on some key issues about the resort are the mayor and city council. You can't think one of them offed her."

"No. First, they wouldn't go by her house. But if someone from work stopped by to talk to her about her opposition to the resort, she'd have let them in, just to be courteous."

George again paused. "Since your rug rats have you busy, and since Morehouse wants Kevin home, I've been asking around."

My mood lifted. "Oh, good. What did you find out?"

"Sandra had no security cameras."

"Nuts."

"The house across the street did. Doesn't show much of her property, but it does show the front porch. The only person who knocked – and went in – about the time she may have been killed was Kevin."

TERRY TEXTED THAT HE would be home after track practice, which resumed today. When he hadn't arrived by six, I began to worry. What if Kevin were the murderer and Terry had found him? I pushed that thought aside. Kevin had been too distraught to have killed Sandra and crafted an alternate story to tell me.

Still, if the guys had gone for pizza or something, Terry would have let us know. Plus, they usually didn't go when they were smelly. Not a good way to impress girls.

My mind jumped to Kevin's girlfriend, Cathy Giacomo. Terry had barely mentioned her the last two days. Was she simply too upset to go to school or help search?

I wanted to talk to Scoobie about what George had said about Kevin being on Sandra's porch, but it would have to be after the twins went to bed. Even assuming Kevin played no role in Sandra's death, I understood Scoobie's concern about us not seeking out Kevin. Maybe Terry should stop looking for him.

Scoobie had started the twins' baths. I finished loading the dishwasher and joined them for what he calls Operation Splashdown.

I stood in the bathroom doorway for several seconds, watching him gently pour water over Leah's hair and add baby shampoo. No one loves being a daddy more than my Scoobie.

Lance spotted me. "Hi, Mommy. If you're good you can come in."

83

With barely room for one adult next to the bathtub, I sat on the closed toilet seat. "I'm very good."

Scoobie turned his head and raised his eyebrows, then went back to the twins. I saw his smile.

Leah shook her head after Scoobie poured rinse water on her hair. "Miss Natalie says there's always room for improvement."

TERRY CAME HOME AT SEVEN Wednesday evening, just in time to say goodnight to the twins. Instead of walking upstairs, he called from downstairs. "Hey, you guys."

Lance yelled, "You better get up here, bub."

Terry laughed and started up the steps.

Was that a second laugh from downstairs?

He stood in the doorway to the twins' room and made a whew gesture across his brow. "Made it in time for a goodnight hug."

Leah stood next to her bed, brushing her head with the back of her hairbrush. "You almost missed us."

Can there be two more self-assured three-year-olds?

I caught Terry's glance at Scoobie before he hugged each twin, and recognized it as a request for a brother confidence. I smiled at the kids. "My turn to turn out the light."

Lance and Leah stared at me, nonplussed, for two seconds, reminding me of Pebbles. "Okay, Mommy," Leah said.

"You can have a turn," Lance added.

It's no secret in our house who the preferred bedtime parent is. I think it has to do with the varied voices Scoobie uses when he reads them stories.

WHEN I CAME DOWNSTAIRS, Kevin's presence in our kitchen wasn't a total surprise. I had figured if anyone could find him, Terry could.

Scoobie had just finished heating up the remains of our stir-fried rice and chicken for the boys. He winked at me.

"I'm sorry I ran from you, Mrs. O'Brien, Mrs. Gentil," Kevin said.

Terry gave me a what-do-I-keep-telling-you look. He wants me to change my last name to O'Brien. Scoobie always tells him he wouldn't recognize me with a different name.

"That car was a scary thing."

Scoobie dumped the food on their plates, and none of us spoke for fifteen seconds or so while the boys took their first bites.

"I don't suppose you saw the driver, did you?" I asked.

"No. Did Uncle Matthew see anything, like on cameras?" Kevin asked.

I shrugged. "Haven't asked him that. Does he know you're here?"

"I told Terry I'd call as soon as we ate."

Ah, to be sixteen and focused on one thing. Well, probably two.

I took my cell phone from the pocket of my slacks and passed it to him.

"Better not." Scoobie grinned. "Morehouse'll accuse you of holding out on him."

"True." I nodded at Kevin. "Yours charged?"

"Um, yeah, but, I was, uh, going to tell them I lost mine. That's why I didn't return their calls."

Terry handed Kevin his phone. I had a feeling that Kevin's mobile provider had worked with the police and let Morehouse know if Kevin had listened to his messages.

Kevin shoveled a couple more bites of food as he dialed his uncle.

Morehouse's gruff voice answered, "You find him, Terry?"

"Uh, yeah, Uncle Matthew. He did."

Who knew Sergeant Morehouse cried?

While we waited for Morehouse and Karen, Scoobie's words came back to me. "A killer knows you found Kevin once. They might follow you and the kids."

What if someone was watching our house now? I excused myself from the kitchen bunch and walked to the front door. Terry had left it unlocked. I locked it.

Before I turned on the porch light, I walked to a closed blind in the living room and carefully lifted one slat. No strange cars on the street.

Red and blue lights bounced off the lamp post in front of the house. Morehouse must have picked up Karen and was using his police lights to get here faster.

A man stood from behind a parked car across the street and jogged into the side street that ran next to that house.

As I unlocked the door, I wrestled with whether to mention the man. He'd be long gone, and he could have been anyone. But stooped behind a car? *Could be a jogger tying his shoes.*

"Kevin. Your family's here."

I opened the door as three people almost toppled out of Morehouse's unmarked car and ran up our porch steps. Scoobie herded them into the kitchen, where the twins were less likely to hear the commotion. I brought in more chairs for our kitchen table.

In a matter of seconds it was clear that Karen and Morehouse were more forgiving of Kevin's absence than his brother was. Brian offered no hugs and stood aside as his mother checked Kevin from head to toe.

Morehouse's eyes sought mine. I shrugged and quietly said, "The boys showed up right before Kevin called you."

Karen turned to Scoobie and me. "Thanks so much."

I said, "Thank Terry, I think."

Brian stood up from the table and leaned across it, toward Kevin. "I'm so mad at you! How could you do that to Mom?"

Kevin recoiled and Morehouse said, "Now Brian, we don't…"

"Don't tell me we don't know what happened. Kevin left and he never called or anything. Mom cried all the time!"

"I'm sorry," Kevin said.

Scoobie said, "Brian."

Brian focused on him.

"You took good care of your mom. Kevin was scared and didn't know what to do. I'm sorry he scared you, too."

I could have kissed my husband. But I wasn't close to him.

Brian deflated and sat down again, tears welling. "Aunt Bella even came."

Karen looked between her sons. "We have a lot to talk about. The important thing is we love each other."

"We do have a lot to talk about," Morehouse said, "but we'll have to have some of that conversation at the station."

"Matthew! Tonight?" Karen asked.

Morehouse hesitated. "I'll call Tortino." He stood and walked into our living room.

When no one said anything, I asked, "Kevin, where did you go after that car, um, seemed to want to hit you?"

He took a deep breath. "I ran under the boardwalk for a few blocks, then I hid there all night. It was pretty cold."

"You weren't under the boardwalk the next day, or someone would have found you," I said.

He nodded. "Um, Cathy's parents don't always lock their windows. I hid in her basement."

Morehouse reentered the kitchen in time to hear the last point. "And you told her you were hiding down there?"

"She would've killed me." He looked at Terry. "Terry, uh, walked around their house and tapped on all the basement windows."

"But not loud," Terry said. "I figured he had to be somewhere where he knew someone."

Karen's eyes brimmed again. "Thank you, Terry."

Terry shrugged. "I kinda think the hard part starts now."

CHAPTER NINE

WE HAD ALL BEEN ENERGIZED by Terry finding Kevin. The two brothers started a rowdy game of chess about nine-thirty, exchanging insults as they claimed the other's chessmen.

Usually one of them does a last-trash-of-the-day dump before bed, but they were having so much fun I took the nearly full garbage bag from under the kitchen sink. I added a couple macaroni and cheese noodles from under the table – where the twins sometimes put them to entice Jazz – and made for the back door.

I yawned broadly as I walked across our small back yard, Jazz at my heels. The Cozy Corner stood tall and dark. Aunt Madge and Harry wore out early these days.

As I closed the lid to the garbage can, Mister Rogers and Miss Piggy began to bark. Sound travels in the quiet. Even though the dogs were inside, their barks and whines carried. "Great. Wake up the neighborhood."

"What do you think, Jazz, should we…"

She hissed loudly, leapt onto our short fence, and dove off toward Aunt Madge's garage.

"Jazz! Come back!"

In an instant I saw where she had aimed herself. The small garage behind the B&B housed Uncle Gordon's boat, which Aunt Madge had never been willing to give away. At first I thought the garage's low-wattage bulb was blinking on and off.

Then I knew. "Fire! Fire! Scoobie!"

Our back door banged open and Terry flew out holding the kitchen fire extinguisher, Scoobie just behind him. I pointed, saying nothing, and opened the back gate so Terry could run next door.

Scoobie ran past, yelling Aunt Madge's address into his phone. "Yes, behind the Cozy Corner. Looks to be a small fire so far."

Someone had to stay near the twins. I stood by our fence, calling for Jazz.

Lights blinked on in the B&B and I could hear Aunt Madge and Harry calling to each other to keep the dogs in as Harry opened the sliding glass door and made toward the garage. He had a larger fire extinguisher.

Terry's voice drifted to me. "I think I got it!"

And then it was dark again.

Scoobie called, "It's okay, Jolie."

"Do you see Jazz?"

Terry laughed. "She's black."

Harry now stood next to Scoobie and Terry. "What happened?"

Aunt Madge had flipped on her large porch light and come outside with the dogs, whom she had on their leashes in the fenced yard. "Where did it start?"

Scoobie bent down to look at something, then stood. "Near where the power comes into the garage."

"Maybe a short," Harry said.

Somehow I didn't think so. Could it have been someone angry at Aunt Madge's campaign goals? Mad at me for asking questions about Sandra's murder? If someone saw me going in and out of the Cozy Corner they might think I lived there, too.

I checked on the sleeping twins and came back outside to hear that the firefighters didn't think an electrical issue had caused the small blaze. As the oldest of them, Mel, explained, "Bunch of rags and newspapers rolled up together, smells like a little bit of charcoal lighter poured on them." He looked at Madge and Harry. "Somebody mad at you folks, or maybe your dogs bark a lot?"

"The dogs are pretty good," Harry said. "Hard to believe someone would do this because of Madge's campaign."

The firefighter named Mel said, "I'd call this a nuisance fire. If someone wanted to hurt you they'd light it closer to the house. Still looks like arson, though."

Aunt Madge said, "There's no way to know if this was aimed at us or if a firebug saw this as a quiet place to ignite something. I will choose to believe the latter unless you tell me otherwise."

Mel nodded. "Not much to go on. Newspaper's charred away, rags look pretty common. We'll get the investigator down here. Take some pictures." He moved back toward his fire department's Honda SUV, the big trucks having left already.

A couple neighbors had called out, but since everything was over so fast, no one else had joined us. The five of us stood together silently, until Scoobie spoke. "Can't do more tonight. I'll find somebody to replace a couple of boards on the side of this old thing." He slapped the garage. "At least the boat wasn't hurt."

Aunt Madge lifted the hem of her terrycloth robe as she turned toward the house. "We can talk tomorrow. In the afternoon."

My foot suddenly felt heavy. Jazz had plopped across my shoe, panting. I picked her up. "Did you chase someone?" I put my head on the top of hers. "If only you could talk."

TERRY HAD FALLEN ASLEEP almost immediately, but Scoobie and I tossed and turned. I was thus not pleased that Lester sent me two text messages before eight Thursday morning. To my knowledge there has never been any such thing as an emergency real estate appraisal. I hoped nothing had happened to Ramona. I called him back.

"I've got a way into the broad's house."

"Lester that sounds like the opening line of a bad crime novel. What are you talking about?"

"See, in Sandra Cartwright's obituary they named her nephew and his wife as her survivors. I called the guy last night."

I groaned. "You mean you asked him to let you list the house? That sounds crass even for your sales sense."

He grunted. "See, I told him I'd do a free walk-through for him. Like an appraisal but not a formal one.

He lives in San Francisco. He don't know the values here. It gets us in her place."

As insensitive as I thought this was, I liked it. "Isn't the house still a crime scene?"

"I called Morehouse this morning. Told him a little white lie, that the guy called me. Said he wanted to set up a real estate contract when he was in town for the funeral. Morehouse said they should finish with the place today."

"Lester, that's more like a big whopper."

He laughed. "See, perfect for me."

I had to smile at his Burger King reference. "Okay. I'm in."

THOUGH MY THOUGHTS WERE on the garage fire, Kevin, and Sandra's death, I had two appraisals to do Thursday. I generally stick to one a day, but with Harry running Aunt Madge's campaign, either I did the work or we would direct the business to Jennifer Stenner's firm. Though we are friendly competitors, sending business to her could mean the bank that asked for the appraisal would go to her first next time.

After dropping the twins at daycare, I first called Aunt Madge.

Her tone was humorous. "Megan called me this morning to say Terry found Kevin."

"I thought it would be too late to call, and I didn't know we'd be meeting in the back yard. I didn't even think about Kevin when we saw the garage fire."

"I'm glad you didn't call. We went to bed at nine because we had a seven A.M. talk today with Rotary." She was silent for several seconds. "As far as I can tell, about the only thing my opponent and I agree on is having a day shelter for homeless people. But even if someone lit that pile of rags because they were angry or disagreed with me, I don't think my opponent, or anyone associated with him, would do such a thing."

I almost smiled. She was becoming a political pro who didn't want to give her adversary attention by using his name. "I suppose I don't think so, either. But maybe it's someone who thinks you, what do people say, want to impede progress?"

I envisioned her shrug. "We can progress without building a monstrosity. Now, you and I need to chat, young lady."

Young lady. She's still mad. "Look, Aunt Madge, I promise, I'll never go anywhere without letting someone know. I'll leave a note on the fridge, or…"

"Pish posh. I mean we need to talk about some things Sandra told me."

I felt irritated. She'd been holding out on me. "Uh, telepathy from the grave?"

"Don't be a smart mouth. I wasn't sure if what she said was relevant. I'm still not. I did tell some of it to Sergeant Morehouse."

"What's your schedule?"

"Packed all day, into evening."

Harry's voice came over the phone. "You can say that again."

Their kiss came through the phone.

"I'm wearing out my husband."

I kept my tone light. "Don't do that. Should I come to the B&B after the twins are in bed this evening?"

"Good idea."

I hung up and headed for the first house to appraise, a bungalow on Seashore Drive. Even driving, I could not get rid of the image of the white garage, dark surrounding it, and flickering light.

I made quick work measuring the rooms and took the interior and exterior photos in less than half an hour. I was at the courthouse looking up comparable sales when Lester texted me. "Meet me at two o'clock at her place."

I said I would, and reminded him I pick up the twins at three so I could hand them to Scoobie and get to the Cozy Corner to serve afternoon tea.

The second house was an older Victorian that had been subdivided into apartments before being taken back to a single-family property. If it hadn't had three kitchens, the renovations would have been less obvious.

It would be a struggle to get the sales contract to support the price the buyer and seller had agreed to. A four-bedroom home sounds big, but two bedrooms weren't much bigger than walk-in closets. The house simply would not normally bring the agreed-upon amount. The buyers wanted the extra kitchens for a mother-in-law and their own teen kids. I would have to be creative in my write-up.

I called Scoobie as I ate a late lunch at home. "All quiet on the hospital front?"

"Couple people heard about our marshmallow roast. I told them we thought it was probably someone who had too much to drink."

"And carries fire starter?"

"I don't mention that."

I MET LESTER AT Sandra's place. Former place. He had already gone in, so I tapped on the screen door and entered. "Hey, Lester."

He came out of the kitchen, diet soda in hand. "Jolie. About time, I…"

"Was that one of Sandra's soft drinks?"

"She can't use 'em. Why'd you park out front instead of in her parking spaces off the alley?"

"Gee, real estate appraisers often use the front door. Why wouldn't I?"

"Come on, we gotta work fast." He shut the door and locked it.

I placed my purse on the solid oak washstand that held a bowl with note paper, pens, keys, and such -- a sort of catch-all table near her front door. "Why do we have to work fast?"

"Told old Morehouse I only needed an hour or less."

I snickered. "You know you're pretty close in age, right?"

"Yeah, but he acts old. I figure you'll make less a mess goin' through the room off the kitchen. Looks like she used it as an office. I'll check out the upstairs bedrooms, and we can do the living room and kitchen together."

"Got it." I strode through the kitchen and stood at the doorway of a tidy home office. A yellow table and chairs in a corner went well with a light-colored desk. Her file cabinet was a vertical one that matched the desk, a far cry from the tall metal ones in Harry's and my office.

Without criteria for a search, I decided to initially skip household paperwork and go for anything that looked hospital-related. The top drawer of her file cabinet was a cross between hospital history and current nursing policies. Nothing jumped out at me.

In addition to files, the bottom drawer held a neat stack of commendations or other awards, a few in frames, most not. "What a career." *And what a waste her death was.*

After searching for ten minutes, I found nothing. I surveyed the room again, and noted that the blotter sat crooked on her desk. I moved a pencil jar from the blotter and peered under it. I hadn't had time to see more than the hospital's name on the hidden letterhead when a car door slammed in the driveway, startling me.

Two sets of footsteps pounded up the front steps. Morehouse yelled, "Lester!" He tried the locked doorknob and rattled it.

Lester hustled down the steps from upstairs. I started to put the letter in my purse, but instead folded it and stuck it in my waist band, between my shirt and underpants, with the belt of my slacks over the shirt. *Have I ever done anything this stupid?*

As Lester opened the front door, I walked into the living room, pulling my notebook from my purse as I did. I hoped my expression was one of practiced nonchalance. Or not practiced. Whichever was more natural.

Morehouse stormed in, followed by the officer who sometimes sat at the station's front desk. "Damn it, Lester, didn't I tell you no snooping?"

"Who the hell is snooping?" Lester asked.

Morehouse pointed at me. "Why is Jolie here?"

I didn't wait for Lester to respond. "What do you think? I appraise real estate for a living. I'm helping Lester establish value for Sandra's nephew." I opened my notebook to the page on which I'd written measurements for the bungalow I'd visited that morning. "Unless you want to take measurements."

Behind Morehouse, I could have sworn the young, red-headed officer rubbed his nose to hide a smile.

Morehouse stared. "Oh. I, uh saw your car and figured you two were up to your old investigating tricks again. This bein' a crime scene."

I frowned. "Lester said you gave permission. And the only *investigating* I've been doing is looking for your nephew."

Morehouse rubbed his hand over his eyes and through his hair. "I'm sorry, Jolie. We've been talking all morning at the station. Some people keep trying to tie Kevin taking off to Sandra's murder."

I almost felt guilty lying. But not quite. "No problem. And he did come back."

Lester, apparently taking cues from me, said, "I didn't see a problem in gettin' Jolie's help."

Morehouse looked at each of us for about three seconds, a long time for a stare. "See anything that makes you think it was more than a burglary?"

"No, I'm thinkin'," Lester began.

"I wasn't looking," I said.

"Oh. Me either," Lester said.

"The corporal and I, oh, you know Corporal Blaine?"

Lester walked the few steps and shook the man's hand, and I gave him a four-finger wave.

Morehouse continued. "We gotta batten down the hatches again. New evidence."

I tried not to seem overly interested. "Are you allowed to say?"

"Yeah, and then after we put the tape up again, I gotta butt out."

Corporal Blaine held up a role of yellow 'do not cross' police tape.

"Why?" I asked.

Morehouse didn't meet my eye as he moved toward Blaine. "Kevin was on Sandra Cartwright's porch the night she was found, and the lab verified that the blood on Kevin's coat is hers. I can't be involved in the death investigation no more."

CHAPTER TEN

MOREHOUSE BEING ANGRY WHEN he thought Lester and I were snooping felt like old times. He was right to suspect us, of course, but I'd never tell him.

Lester and I stood on the sidewalk after Morehouse and Corporal Blaine started putting up the yellow crime scene tape. "Look at my notebook, Lester."

He took the cigar out of his mouth. "Why?"

"Because we're supposed to be coming up with a suggested value for this house, and we need to look like we're discussing it."

"Oh, yeah." He put the unlit cigar at the corner of his mouth and nodded at where I pointed to a page. "Just gimme a number."

I rolled my eyes. "I'll send you an email after I do the tea at the Cozy Corner. You send me a note back agreeing, or disagreeing."

"Why?"

"Is that your new word? It'll show we followed through on figuring out a listing price."

Lester jingled the car keys in his pocket. "Guess it was good for something."

Morehouse and Blaine had gone back into the house. "Maybe two things. I found a letter under her desk blotter."

Jingling stopped and Lester moved so his back was to the house and he faced me. "What'd it say?"

"Don't know. I hid it."

He jerked a thumb over his shoulder, toward the house. "In there?"

"On me. I'll read it and call you."

"Uh uh. Dibbsies. I got us in there."

I smiled. "It's not where I can easily pull it out."

Lester's cigar fell to the sidewalk and he stooped to retrieve it.

I turned toward my car. "I'll call you, and then make you a copy."

"Hubba, hubba."

THOUGH I HAD MOVED THE folded letter into my purse, I had no time to read it until I cleared empty bread plates and teacups at the Cozy Corner. I'd been lucky to pick up the kids at daycare before I had to pay a premium for collecting them more than five minutes late.

I let the dogs into the great room, poured myself a lukewarm cup of tea, and sat at the large oak table in Madge and Harry's kitchen area.

I had not expected a letter of resignation.

Dear Mr. Wharton and members of the board,

All employees, especially the most senior, must implement – or at least support -- leadership decisions with dedication, even enthusiasm. I cannot support the board's decision to propose that the hospital's endowment fund invest a substantial portion of its resources in the resort's development. I strongly believe this choice to be a risky one that, over time, could affect the quality of care the hospital can provide.

It is thus with profound regret that I tender my resignation to the Ocean Alley Hospital Board of Directors.

The next few paragraphs referenced what she considered positive changes of the last few years and thanked a couple of board members by name. Given that the date was that of her death, she could have finished it just before she was killed. She hadn't printed it at the hospital, because she didn't work the day before her body was found.

I studied the letter again and realized it bore no signature. What did that mean? Did the killer have the signed original?

Lester had the same question when I called him.

"We have to get this to the police, Lester. But I don't know how."

"Should we mail it to 'em, ya think?"

"Maybe," I hesitated. "You still have the key to her place?"

"Since it's you, I'll say I made a copy. Why?"

I inwardly cringed. A key he shouldn't have, and I was suggesting he use it. "Why don't you put the letter back? Under the blotter."

"You forget about the crime tape?"

"I remember. I give you the letter. You Xerox it, but wear gloves when you pick up the copy. Go back to her place at night, and put it under the blotter."

"You gonna visit me in the hoosegow?"

I smiled. "I'll bake you a pie and put a switchblade in it."

"A hack saw, dummy." He sighed. "All right. Better do it tonight. Where are you?"

"Come to Aunt Madge's now, would you? I don't want Scoobie to know I ever had this."

Not until I finished fixing dinner two hours later did I consider that the returned letter would have no prints on it, not even Sandra's. Morehouse would notice that and come straight to me.

I RARELY GO OUT after we put the kids to bed, so I had to be honest with Scoobie about why Aunt Madge and I needed to talk Thursday evening.

He yawned. "They can come over here."

I grinned. "You just want to listen."

"Her I trust."

When he then raised an eyebrow, I added, "I think they're really whipped."

"I forget she's in her eighties and he's late seventies."

I nodded. "Me, too. Leave a note about what you want to have for lunch tomorrow, and I'll pack you one." He loves it when I make his lunch. I think it's because his mother never did. Not that he sees me as a mother figure.

He wrote out his menu preferences before I left, and I blew him a kiss as I shut the door behind me. The warmth of the eight-thirty evening temperature surprised me. Perhaps we really had moved to summer at the beginning of May.

I pressed the security code and walked into Aunt Madge's side door at eight-thirty-five. "Hey you two."

As I started for the swinging door into the great room, she came out, finger over her lips. "Harry's already sawing logs. Too much excitement last night." She pointed to her electric kettle as she settled at one of the guest breakfast tables with her already-poured cup.

I poured myself a mug of hot water and added a teabag. "Did you hear anything else from the fire department?"

She shook her head. "Don't expect to. Someone told Paul Holley about it. He called to say he was sorry it happened and that someone had stolen half of his yard signs a few days ago. Probably pranksters."

"Pranksters steal signs, they don't set fires."

"It's out of my control. I thought it was good of my opponent to call."

I suppressed a smile. Back in campaign mode. "How's the battle going?"

"We're getting more requests to talk to groups since I was on that morning radio program a few days ago."

"Was that the show where you said kids who walk to school would have to be sure to stay away from the resort part of town to avoid drunk drivers?"

She grinned. "I didn't initiate that part of the conversation. But I did raise the point with the interviewer before we went on the air."

I took out the tea bag and tossed it into the table-top trash can before I sat opposite her. "And you say I'm devious."

She sombered. "I don't know all of Sandra's concerns, but some of them were with the hospital's reasons for wanting the resort."

I wasn't about to admit I'd seen that letter. "More people in town could mean more patients. Was she concerned about taxing hospital staff or something?"

"From the last conversation we had, it seemed she had heard the developer wasn't getting the level of capital he needed. He wanted some of the hospital's endowment fund. Not to keep, as an investment."

"And she had a problem with that?"

"She inferred there was a kind of quid pro quo aspect to it. The developer would donate to the hospital later. She didn't understand why the board would even consider recommending that the Endowment Committee make that investment."

My ex was a banker, and when I was a commercial real estate agent, we talked a fair bit about finances. "Endowment managers usually make pretty conservative investments. I wouldn't expect them to invest in something that could be precarious."

I thought for another moment. I didn't want the resort, but it didn't seem overly risky. "I can't think of any big hotels on our part of the shore that have gone under in more than a decade. What was she worried about?"

"Can you say hurricane?" Aunt Madge asked, dryly.

I almost smiled. She bought her B&B on D Street because she wouldn't buy any closer to the shore. A hurricane in the 1940s took out the boardwalk and A

Street, and she wanted to reduce the odds of losing her business.

"Also cyclone. But wouldn't there be insurance? And anyway, once the resort was up and running, the hospital endowment would get some, or all of its investment back, yes?"

Aunt Madge shrugged. "Supposedly. Sandra was more concerned with why Quentin Wharton and a couple board members were so anxious to 'grow the hospital,' as they said. She thought someone might have a personal stake in the investment decision, but she couldn't find one."

I chose my words carefully. "Sometimes younger people favor growth, in any industry, more than people who have worked in a place for a while."

"Mind your mouth, gal." But she smiled.

I stared into my teacup. "Funny that developer guy wants to buy Mr. Markle's store if he's short on funds."

Aunt Madge slopped her tea. "What? We can't lose the store! It's the only place downtown to buy groceries."

"Gee, if you don't know, maybe I shouldn't have mentioned that Jack Borman guy talked to him. Mr. Markle hasn't made up his mind."

Aunt Madge put her elbow on the table and a hand to her forehead.

She rarely appears distressed. "I'm so sorry to upset you…"

"You aren't the problem." She removed her hand and gave me a grim smile. "This time. We have to think of something."

Plotting with Aunt Madge? What dimension is this? "You mean like have a lot of people tell Mr. Markle what he means to us? I don't know what Harvest for All would do without him."

She shook her head. "Not that. I'll sound out Mr. Markle. We need to know more about this developer and why he thinks he wants funds from sources at the hospital. If this Jack Borman can afford to buy more property than in his original proposal to the city, he can leave the hospital alone."

I snapped my fingers. "We can start a scholarship fund in Sandra's name. Or collect for something the nurses want at the hospital."

Aunt Madge's eyebrows went up and then she frowned. She looked as if she thought I was sleep-deprived, like right after the twins were born.

I grinned. "The one thing I've learned running Harvest for All is that almost any bigwig in town will talk to you about donating to a charity. As long as you give them credit."

SCOOBIE WAS STILL UP WHEN I got home. He loved the idea of dedicating a scholarship or raising money to donate an item in Sandra's name. He even volunteered to talk to some people at the hospital to get ideas for a project that would have been meaningful to her.

I halfway felt bad that Aunt Madge and I had come up with the idea as a way for me to get to Jack Borman. We thought he might throw her out of his office. Scoobie didn't have to know what we were up to to be glad about the donation idea.

Did Borman have a local office? Before I got ready for bed, I began an online search for Jack Borman's business address.

Lester called as I searched. "Good of you to check on me, kid."

I'd actually forgotten our plan to sneak the letter back into Sandra's house. "You would have called me for bail money if you needed it."

He snorted. "I put it under her blotter thing about ten tonight. You really think some shenanigans at the hospital got her killed?"

I decided to be evasive. "Seems a long shot. I might call George to see what he thinks."

"Oh, yeah, call good old George."

Lester and George barely tolerate each other. I think it's because in some ways they are too similar. "I'll tell him you said hello."

SANDRA'S FUNERAL WAS SCHEDULED for eleven Friday morning, at First Prez. I planned to accompany Aunt Madge and Harry. Scoobie said so many people at the hospital wanted to attend that he didn't ask for the time off.

As we enjoyed three minutes of quiet before the twins were up, I reread Sandra's obituary. In the past, I thought little when I saw someone had no children. Now, I felt as if Sandra had been cheated twice. No close family and an early death.

"What are you thinking?" Scoobie asked.

I tapped the paper. "She had a nephew. Lester talked to him, to suggest that he'd go through the house and give the guy an idea of what to list it for."

Scoobie snorted. "Good for Lester."

I wasn't about to say Lester actually had a good motive, though it had nothing to do with easing the nephew's pain. "I don't think he tied his offer to securing the listing."

Scoobie looked at me over a glass of juice. "Did Lester grow a new soul?"

I threw a Cheerio at him, then sobered. "I hate funerals."

"At least you aren't in the casket." He put a banana peel in the trash. "Come on, time to help the kidlets start another day of havoc."

I LEFT A MESSAGE for George as soon as I dropped off the kids and made it to the appraisal office. All appraisal requests, except Lester's, are electronic or start with a call that's forwarded to my cell.

Harry and I hope Lester's fax machine eventually wears out. Aside from having to be sure to check our machine regularly, when he doesn't like the appraisal results Lester writes insulting notes. Usually he directs them to Harry.

When George didn't call back in half-an-hour, I tried again. Ramona answered.

"Gosh, Ramona, did I dial you by mistake?"

"Oops. Morning, Jolie. Just a sec." In a muffled voice, she said, "Sorry, I picked up the wrong phone."

Oh. My. God.

"Hey, Jolie, I was about to call you back."

I glanced at my watch. Just after nine A.M. I raised my voice. "Sleeping late?"

In the background, Ramona laughed.

"You're as funny as an empty print cartridge," he said.

Ramona laughed some more.

I took mercy on George. "Aunt Madge talked to Sandra about some people at the hospital wanting to invest part of its endowment fund in the resort. I thought we could look into that after the funeral."

"Huh. The hospital Endowment Committee is separate from its governing board. I think Sandra was a voting member of the endowment one."

I slapped my forehead. We'd been talking about the two hospital entities, but I'd forgotten that endowments were always independent. "Sandra really did have a strong say in whether that money went to the resort."

Ramona called from some distance from George's phone. "I'm heading over to the gallery."

"So you guys sleep at your place?"

"Criminy, Jolie. I gotta call you back." George hung up.

I SPENT TIME ONLINE LOOKING for houses that would support the sales price for the Victorian with three kitchens. Though the request had come from a local bank, the agent who inked the deal was Lester. I would never overstate a house's value for an appraisal. On the other hand, I had suggested Lester enter a crime scene without permission.

George returned my call as I was about to leave for the courthouse for some more in-depth research.

"Jolie, I don't want any snide comments."

"So, nothing about sleepovers or wedding bells?"

George swore loudly.

I suppressed a giggle. "Gosh, I hope you aren't at Java Jolt."

George was done playing games. "Whaddya know?"

I outlined Sandra's conversation with Aunt Madge, and made it sound as if she told me about Sandra's planned resignation rather than me finding the letter in her house. I trusted George, but if he ever let that slip, Scoobie would be furious. And he would probably have a right to be.

"Did you talk to Scoob about this? He can put his ear to the ground at the hospital."

"We are talking about my husband, right? Mister What-Happens-In-Vegas-Stays-in-Vegas?"

George snorted. "More like he learns from the mistakes of others."

"Huh?"

"An AA slogan. He's seen you step in it. He can pay attention without butting in."

I remembered the letter of reprimand, but even I knew that was Scoobie's business to talk to George about, not mine. "He can listen, but he rarely leaves Radiology." I wanted to get off the Scoobie topic. "Do you know who's on that Endowment Committee or Board?"

"I do. You'll love one of them. Your old pal Dr. Welby."

Dr. Welby, who tells people he had the name before the television show, was on the Harvest for All Committee for years. I relied on him heavily my first couple of years. He had a way of advising without making you feel dumb not to know something already.

"Okay. I'll call him. Who else?"

"Couple other docs, Mr. Greentree at the bank, a health sciences professor at the community college – I don't know her – and, of course, Sandra Cartwright was a member."

I didn't want to work the committee on my own. "Who will you talk to?"

"First, I'm going to ask the editor if I can do a feature article on all the ways the resort would affect the community."

"Why? Oh, it gives people a reason to talk to you."

"Yep. He'll say yes. Tiffany hates to write features. Then I'll head over to the bank."

Since I had no flour on my hands, I decided to do a pen-and-paper to-do list.

- Call Dr. Welby for background on endowment use
- Courthouse research
- Get on Borman's schedule about Harvest for All
- Kevin on Sandra's porch
- Call Morehouse re person Kevin saw in at Sandra's

I'd thought so much about the hospital's potential financial support for the resort that I'd almost forgotten about Kevin. Did anyone really think his presence on Sandra's porch meant that he'd killed her?

CHAPTER ELEVEN

I KNOW SOME PEOPLE who go to visitations and funerals almost as a social event. I hate both. Fortunately, Sandra's nephew chose to have people visit at First Prez before the funeral rather than the night before.

The parking lot overflowed. I dropped off Aunt Madge and Harry and parked a block and a half from the red brick church. As I walked back I took in its traditional white steeple and wondered if a developer would someday want the property. I remembered Reverend Jamison once telling me the congregation had an offer to buy the site. They turned it down.

Norman Cartwright and his wife Annette seemed like solemn folks, even considering their reason for being in town. When Madge, Harry, and I made it through the line to them, I felt as if I was shaking hands with store mannequins. Very tall and proper.

Though Norman did not signal a need for familiarity, Aunt Madge hugged him as she introduced herself. "Sandra Cartwright was a delightful person. I'm sorry you won't have her anymore."

"Ah. She mentioned you and your campaign." He smiled slightly. "She seemed to think you would be Ocean Alley's Savior Mayor."

Harry put a fist over his mouth as he cleared his throat, but I knew he was hiding a smile. I didn't meet his eyes.

"Goodness," Aunt Madge said, "I'll have to work even harder."

Norman and Annette sat in the front row by themselves, which seemed lonely to me. The second row looked like a military line-up of hospital senior staff, with Quentin Wharton seated by the aisle. All men, except the director of human resources, and all in black.

Sandra was to be cremated, but I didn't see an urn anywhere. Maybe the medical examiner hadn't even released her body. *Ugh.*

Reverend Jamison had a lot of good things to say about Sandra, many of which I didn't know. He thought about half the nurses at the hospital had met her via career days at various high schools, and come to Ocean Alley Hospital because of her. "Filling her shoes may be possible, but it's hard to imagine anyone as dedicated as the hospital's late director of nursing."

As the service ended, I noted Sergeant Morehouse in a back pew. He had on a suit rather than his more casual detective clothes. He also wore no badge. I figured he was on his own time. Or checking out people and not wanting to look obvious. When others began to walk down the steps to the community room for lunch, I walked back to Morehouse.

I sat next to him. "Nice to see you."

"She was good to Kevin."

I nodded. "Do you mind if I ask you…"

He grunted, "What are my choices?"

I smiled. "Not a hard question. I know that car seemed to be aiming for Kevin, but I thought it was pretty scary, too. Do you have any idea who drove it or what kind of car it was?"

He shook his head. "And we been sayin' for years that we need more cameras downtown. People always think we're going to use 'em as speed traps and the damn city council won't appropriate money for 'em."

"Maybe you can lobby the next mayor."

That got a smile. "Maybe I will."

The church community room was packed for lunch. Expecting a large crowd, First Prez had accepted food donations but also ordered trays of sandwiches, along with chips and cookies.

I stopped at the table of hospital staff and stood next to Wharton. "I'm sure this is a sad day for you all."

Everyone, including Scoobie's boss, Sam, murmured in agreement. When no one said anything else, I nodded and went back to Aunt Madge.

From where I sat near the table of lemonade and coffee, I watched the hospital contingent. I would have expected them to be talking about Sandra, maybe sharing stories, some of which could be funny. They ate in near silence.

Were they all angry at her for opposing Wharton's support for the resort? Or didn't they want to let the man know how much they had cared about her?

WORK HAD TO COME first when the twins were in daycare, so even though I was emotionally tired after the funeral, I headed for the courthouse. The cloudless blue sky and light breeze did not encourage indoor work. Fortunately, temps would also rise to the low eighties, very warm for the shore in May. Air conditioning would beckon at that point.

Within half-an-hour I found two houses similar to the Victorian that would let me support the price in the sales contract. Both were more elegantly presented, but they had similar square footage and four bedrooms. I decided to use the three kitchens as enhancements to value.

At the courthouse I also found Jack Borman's contact information. He had placed it on a Power Point document he presented to the Ocean Alley City Council.

The presentation said Shoreline Investments planned to build the Ocean View Resort "along Ocean Alley's magnificent shoreline." They expected to add almost 300 jobs, but most part-time, and promised to be a "responsible member of the Ocean Alley business and community teams." *Teams? Every guy wants a sports analogy.*

I sat on a bench outside the Office of the Registrar of Deeds to think. I wanted to talk to Dr. Welby as a member of the hospital's Endowment Committee and to Borman about the resort's finances, though I probably couldn't use such a direct phrase. Who first?

I would probably get straight facts from Dr. Welby. Him first.

Dr. Welby often mentions visiting 'the club.' In movies that usually means a wood-paneled bastion in the center of a large city, with lots of mixed drinks on the rocks. In Ocean Alley people, mostly men, mean a nine-hole golf course just west of town proper. Its small clubhouse serves cold beer and burgers.

The young man in the pro shop, the only staff member I've ever seen outside of the bar, told me Dr. Welby had just finished a round of golf and would likely grab a bite before he left. I wandered into the bar and stared, unseeing, out the large picture window at the first hole.

I couldn't help but think about Kevin. His only link to poor Sandra's death was finding the body. Because he had taken off for a couple of days, he was definitely getting a look by the police. Who else were they considering?

Sandra's small but well-maintained house was in one of the nicer parts of town. A thief could have planned a break-in, not expecting her to be home. Her purse and some jewelry were missing, but why take only those if the only person who could stop you was dead on the floor?

If her non-voting role on the hospital governing board and voting position on the Endowment Committee were strong enough to discourage requested investment in the resort, people could be angry. But how many developers or town leaders would be willing to kill to get her out of the way?

My sense was none. Her death could have been an accident. Someone went there to persuade her and they argued. Still pretty far-fetched.

But only Kevin was seen on her front porch. I thought of the small, wooden garage and extra parking space behind her house, typical of older Ocean Alley neighborhoods. Someone she knew could have parked there and come to her back door. Nothing I saw in her house gave the impression of recent repairs because of forced entry. She probably let her attacker in through that door near her garage.

Behind me, Dr. Welby boomed, "Jolie. What a nice surprise."

Even in a place where casual dress was the norm, Dr. Welby was groomed precisely. He wore tan slacks with creases and a collared, yellow shirt rather than the typical polo style golfers usually sported.

I walked to him and kissed his cheek. "You look fit."

Dr. Welby glanced to the man behind the bar. "The usual for me and," he pointed a finger at me.

"Iced tea would be great."

"Tea for my friend. On my account." He gestured to one of the small, round tables. Two others across the room were occupied, but I didn't worry about being overheard.

"Did you have a good round?" I asked.

"If you mean did I enjoy it, absolutely. We won't talk score."

I nodded. "I'm looking for some background information. On Sandra."

His jovial expression vanished. "Heck of a thing. One of the best nurses—best people—I've known."

"She and Aunt Madge were good friends. My interest is because Terry's good friend, Kevin, stopped by that night and found her. He's upset, as you might…"

"I don't remember reading that."

"Hasn't been in the paper yet. In fact, he was so unnerved he took off for a couple days."

"Ah. That kid. Small note in the paper today simply said he had returned home and his mother thanked people for their help. I figured he was a runaway."

"Perhaps in the sense that he left voluntarily, but it was because he was shook up. Not a fight at home or anything like that."

"Knew Sandra well, did he?"

"Only recently." I launched into an abbreviated version of what Kevin had heard in the recovery room and that he'd sought out Sandra because he knew she was Madge's friend. "She had jokingly told him she was probably the nurse the men were mad at. He saw her letter to the editor the day of her death. I guess he wanted to touch base with her."

"You believe him?"

"I do. He's Terry's best friend, and a good kid. Like the cop shows say, he'd have no motive to kill her."

The server brought my tea and Dr. Welby's coffee, plus half of a bagel with scrambled eggs on it for him.

"My wife regulates my egg intake. Don't tell on me." He took a generous bite. "Best food here."

"So, to really get Kevin off the hook, I'd like to know who killed her and whether it had anything to do with the proposal for a resort."

He paused with coffee halfway to his mouth. "Quite a leap there."

I nodded. "I asked a couple of innocuous questions at the hospital, and almost immediately Scoobie gets some reprimand letter. If that hadn't happened, I'd probably be more willing to let go."

He downed a big gulp of coffee. "And Scoobie had no reason to expect such a letter?"

"No. His boss thought it was odd, too."

"Hmm. Well, I don't really know anyone in personnel there," he began.

"Scoobie will deal with that in his own way. I know you and Sandra were on the Endowment Committee together. I'm not sure who planted the idea with George, but he seems to think Jack Borman wanted the committee to approve investing some of the endowment in the resort project."

He shook his head. "So much for closed meetings and confidentiality."

"So it's true? They're short on cash?"

"Could be. Or maybe we were one of fifty groups Mr. Borman and others contacted because they didn't want to tie up all their capital."

"And do you think the committee would have approved the investment?"

"A couple members were receptive, but Sandra chaired our group and she was bitterly opposed to the idea. Said it was riskier than betting on a vaccine for the common cold."

"And, uh, with her gone, is there a better chance that the endowment fund will invest?"

He shrugged. "I suppose the resort could make another pitch. They might think they have a chance, but I'd say no. Most of us have known each other for a while. I think that after her death, a yes vote would leave a bitter taste."

"So Sandra's opposition was the only reason you folks voted no?"

Dr. Welby wiggled his hand, palm down, above the table. "We usually do pick conservative options -- bonds and money market funds."

Before I could ask another question, he changed the subject. "Now, tell me how the fundraiser is shaping up for this weekend."

Discussion ended.

I CALLED JACK BORMAN'S office. I fully expected to be told he could not spare time for the chair of Harvest for All, but his secretary penciled me in, her term, for two-fifty that afternoon.

Rats. I'll have to pay overtime at daycare. I called Scoobie to ask if he'd pick up the kids at three-fifteen, because I had a meeting. Then I let the daycare know the twins would be there an additional half-hour.

Since the fundraiser was the next day, Scoobie didn't even ask what meeting. Lucky break.

I'd have time to go directly to the Cozy Corner to serve tea. When I called George to tell him about the appointment, he begged to come with me. "Just tell him you mentioned it to me in Java Jolt, and I said I was doing the feature article."

"He'll throw us out."

George's impatience came through. "I'll tell him I'm starting with him to give the resort the best possible angle."

"Do people fall for lines like that?"

"Depends on how much their public and private agendas differ."

I thought about that for a moment. "Meaning if they're trying to pull the wool over someone's eyes they're more anxious to explain how transparent they are?"

"Bingo," George said.

I HAD TIME TO MAKE a bunch of phone calls on behalf of the fundraiser before getting to Jack Borman's office. Scoobie and I are less hands-on at those events since the twins arrived. Reverend Jamison at First Prez, and Father Teehan at George's church, St. Anthony's, didn't want the pantry to slow down, so they each found a few more volunteers. More like goaded, according to George, who was put into service.

I sat in Java Jolt to make the calls. A flower shop in town had ordered hundreds of latex balloons for us. They donated them as long as we paid for the helium tank. The balloon order had come in.

Harry usually runs the balloon giveaway so half the town's teenagers, and a few adults, don't do helium hits to make their voices high for a short time. Harry enlisted Max to help.

We hadn't planned as much food because we weren't charging admission and boardwalk vendors would be on hand with their products. We'd hired a local food truck to make and sell tacos for only fifty cents. We'd pay the vendor an additional fifty cents. My fingers were crossed that a lot of attendees would put money in the taco donation jar.

Ice cream cones would be free between two and four. We'd collected money for ice cream donations for weeks. I hoped weekend temps were cooler than today's so people would eat less cold stuff.

JACK BORMAN'S TEMPORARY SPACE in the Beachcomber's Alley Hotel had a great view of the ocean. His persona and very expensive suit implied that any office he worked in should be the best. With gold rims and his company's crest, even the thermos of coffee and two mugs on his desk radiated wealth.

George's presence was not a preferred component of his realm. He minced no words saying so.

"Listen," George said. "Jolie mentioned she was going to talk to you and I'm about to start this feature on all aspects of the resort. But I can head out and you can have one of your staff call me. No problem."

I suspected Borman knew that if George left he would depict Borman as the developer who threw out an inquiring mind. If he'd known George better, he might have still done better ejecting George.

When we seemed to have agreement that George would stay, I began. "I know you don't actually live in Ocean Alley…"

"But I do know the community well," Borman said.

I smiled. "That wasn't an editorial comment. I want to familiarize you with the food pantry I chair, and suggest our Cinco de Mayo festival this weekend would be a good way to meet a lot of people."

He settled in his high-backed leather chair and picked a piece of lint from the arm of his wool suit. "At this hotel? When the resort is finished you'll have a lot more options."

"On the boardwalk, extending from the kiddie rides area going six blocks or so north."

"You looking for a donation?"

"Always welcome," I said, "but not specifically. A lot of community groups and nonprofits have fun booths. They donate some of what they bring in. Even the hospital has a presence."

Before Borman could say anything, George jumped in. "Jolie roped me into helping with Harvest for All, but I thought you might want to describe your vision for the resort, and how you think Ocean Alley will benefit."

Borman frowned. "Who are you writing this for?"

"*Ocean Alley Press*. I worked there years ago, and still do some stories now and then."

"What do you do now?"

"I was an insurance investigator for a couple years, now I head a general investigation firm."

Head?

"Divorce and stuff?" Borman asked.

George grinned. "Only if I can't avoid it. Still a lot of insurance work, track down long-lost family members after someone dies. Anything legal anyone will pay me to do."

Borman seemed to decide that George would be a good tool for his vision. He talked nonstop for five minutes about luxury accommodations, two pools – one indoor, one outdoor – fabulous restaurants, and job opportunities for "a depressed economy."

Depressed economy? Ocean Alley had come out of the recession pretty well.

I tuned out and glanced around his office. All hotel furniture had been removed, replaced with his large desk, probably maple, matching credenza, a small conference table, and several very expensive-looking guest chairs. He'd also added a couple of area rugs that I guessed hid the kinds of stains that litter the carpet of older hotels.

Definitely a room designed to impress.

George cleared his throat. "Jolie?"

"Oh, sorry. I was admiring your office and working on my mental to-do list for the fundraiser."

Borman did not appear pleased at my lack of attention.

"Jolie here used to be in commercial real estate, so I may sound naïve…"

"Here?" Borman asked. "I may have an opening if we add condos."

Add condos! "I sold real estate in Lakewood. Before I had my three-year-old twins. My schedule is a little too crazy to sell real estate these days." I hoped my smile hid my shock at hearing he wanted to add condos.

"So," George said, "How do you get financing for something this big? I mean, it can't be your only project. Or is it?"

Borman almost bristled. "Shoreline Investments has a range of real estate development and property management projects."

George's smile might be called ingratiating. Or one that implied big boys know how things work.

"So, you must have lines of credit out the ying yang."

Borman glanced away and back. For the first time, he had a kind of cagey expression. "We do like to provide some local investment opportunities."

"Any in this area?" George asked.

Borman reached into the breast pocket of his suit. He held up his index finger, letting us know he had something important to attend to, pulled out his phone, and glanced at his screen. After a few seconds, he said, "Sorry folks. I'm going to have to run back to meet one of my colleagues in a few minutes."

He stood, and George and I both reached across his desk to shake hands. "Thanks so much for letting us talk to you," I said. "Another time, I'd like to see if you'd be interested in making a small donation for something at the hospital, in memory of Sandra Cartwright."

He shook his head as he came from behind his desk. "So sad. You're welcome to call."

In a fluid motion he guided us to the door. "Come back anytime."

Over my shoulder, as he was shutting the door, I called, "Think about coming to the boardwalk Saturday."

We bade goodbye to his secretary in her tiny vestibule space, and headed for the elevator. Neither George or I said anything until we were back in fresh air. I breathed deeply.

"You noted when he threw us out, right?" George asked.

"As soon as we talked money. I'd say there's a guy who's strapped for cash."

AS BART MOBLEY LINGERED OVER HIS bread and tea, I did dishes from the other guests and wiped Aunt Madge's counters. I could hear him puttering around the guest breakfast room, so I sat at the kitchen table and dialed Morehouse's cell phone.

He answered on the second ring. "Hey, Jolie. Listen, I'm sorry I blew up at you yesterday. Hadn't even heard about that fire thing at Madge's."

It sounded as if he would say more, and I didn't deserve an apology. He was right to figure Lester and I were up to something in Sandra's house. "No biggie. We haven't heard anything else about the fire."

"I'll letcha know if I do."

"I'm calling to check on Kevin, but didn't want to trouble Karen if she was dealing with a lot."

"She's tough, but his shook her up," Morehouse said.

"We're all thrilled he's safe. He talked to me quite a bit while we sat in the salt water taffy place. I've been meaning to ask if you know who he saw next to Sandra's house. I never read anything about it."

"No. We're keepin' it outta the media for now. What Kevin remembers most are his eyes. Too dark to tell the color, but he said they kind of bore into him. Whatever the hell that means."

"I'm sorry he had that experience."

"Aren't we all. It'll be a long time before he gets over findin' Sandra Cartwright's body."

"Will he go to a… never mind. Not my business."

"Yeah, a counselor. Quentin Wharton at the hospital called the day after we found, Terry found, Kevin. Suggested a couple folks. One's a psychologist, can't remember what the other is."

"Boy, that was really thoughtful." *Does Wharton hope a counselor would tell him what Kevin says?*

"Meant the world to my sister."

We lapsed into what novelists call a pregnant pause.

I ended it. "Are you any closer to figuring out what happened to Sandra?"

"Told you I'm on the outs for that, but the short answer is no. Far as I've heard."

I picked an imagined speck of dirt from Aunt Madge's table. "No one really suspects Kevin, do they?"

Morehouse grunted. "Don't think so. With the blood on his sleeve and him looking panicked when he came out her front door…Did you know the neighbor had a security camera that showed Sandra's front porch?"

"If you won't kill the messenger, George told me."

He snorted. "Lady who had the camera's been telling everyone she's helping us. Best point for him is that he was in there less than a minute, and he didn't leave with her purse."

"What a relief."

"You tell George, he picks up anything call me. Or Tortino, I guess."

CHAPTER TWELVE

THE SATURDAY OF CINCO de Mayo dawned bright and pleasantly warm. Not too hot.

Though the fundraiser didn't start until noon, I was up at five. On days like this I wish we had an au pair. I suppose even if we did, the twins wouldn't want to be handed off to someone else. They seem to be able to sense a good time and always want to be in on it.

I finished printing a slew of volunteer name badges.

Scoobie sleeps until seven on Saturday morning, which means he gets up when the kids do. I made our traditional Saturday meal of pancakes and turkey bacon. Terry is not a fan of rising early on the weekends, but the smell of bacon always brings him to the table.

By eight-thirty, the five of us were out the door. My plan was to join Ramona on the boardwalk and put up signs while Scoobie and Terry helped the vendors and other groups set up their tables or booths.

The twins would want to be out of their stroller, but I also knew they would be worn out by ten-thirty and ready to go home for a nap with Scoobie. He would bring them back when they woke up, which would probably be about the time the festival started at noon.

When we got to the boardwalk, Aunt Madge already had the bake sale table set up with a couple dozen plates of cookies, cupcakes, and chocolate pretzels. Harvest for All board member Monica was her always-nervous self and had managed to drop a plate of snickerdoodles. Our rule is that anything that hits the ground is fair game for volunteers -- as long as it didn't stay on the floor, or in this case the boardwalk, for more than a few seconds.

Karen, Kevin, and Brian would spend part of the afternoon helping in the salt water taffy store. Mr. Fitzpatrick planned to donate half of the retail price of a box of candy to Harvest for All. I was glad that Kevin wanted to be out and about, but still concerned because we didn't know who had seemingly tried to run him down.

I visited every business and booth before starting time. Ramona had made signs for participating boardwalk businesses and any booth that would set up on the boardwalk. The signs said *gold plated donor*, and featured our Harvest for All logo and an open can of corn lying on its side.

Instead of corn, gold coins came out. Each one said something different. They had phrases such as thank you for helping, breakfast is the best, food helps learning, and volunteers always welcome.

I stopped at Ramona's booth, admiring the many pen-and-ink drawings she had specifically created to sell for Harvest for All. With her long, blonde hair and usual multi-colored clothes that I think of as gauzy, she looked like a hippy.

She grinned. "Good thing I draw fast."

"I'm always amazed. Thanks for donating so many."

She gestured to a jar of colorful pencils and a sketch pad. "I'm going to do quick drawings for people who donate more than ten dollars. It'll be good advertising for my gallery."

I winked at her. "Do one of George for Scoobie and me."

She blushed. "We're having fun."

I moved to a booth full of beach souvenirs. In addition to the usual assortment of fans, crabs made from shells, pens saying Ocean Alley, and pennants, there were dozens of hard plastic coffee mugs with beach scenes. The idea of drinking coffee on the beach did not appeal to me, though I could have used a cup now.

Most of the businesses planned to donate a percentage of their sales. Some also had baskets of goods to raffle. Mr. Markle had a bunch of grocery store gift cards to give to anyone who brought more than ten cans or other items of food.

The idea of collecting, boxing, and then transporting the items to Harvest for All had not thrilled me. However a bunch of Alicia's college friends had volunteered to handle that. I was trying to figure out how to get their names so I could call them to see if they wanted to volunteer at other times.

The hospital booth was primarily a source of information, though they did have the donation bucket if people wanted to chip in for the small coloring books for kids. I was surprised to see Quentin Wharton himself with the hospital's usual publicity guru and a pediatric nurse. Nurses in their pastel scrubs sporting teddy bears and kittens are a draw at any event the hospital hosts or participates in. Quentin not so much.

When I walked up to say hello about eleven-forty-five, Quentin's hello was cooler than the ocean in May.

"Hello Jolie. I thought I would give people a chance to see that the hospital CEO isn't interested simply in commercial development."

I swallowed, glad Scoobie wasn't with me. "I know for a fact that Aunt Madge never used those words to describe you. She was talking generally about businesses being more concerned with their bottom lines then continuing what she calls a cohesive community."

"I read her interviews."

I was not about to debate him.

"Will some other board members be here?" I asked.

"I believe a couple are coming about two."

"I hope you enjoy talking to people and reach some of the folks you want to target."

Quentin's expression seemed to say he was very much in charge and didn't need my good wishes.

I stopped at several booths to thank vendors or community groups. A group of interfaith volunteers had people from every church that provided volunteers – or sent needy people to – Harvest for All. Father Teehan was happily debating something with the Unitarian minister, and an older woman holding a rosary looked scandalized.

Both men waved. "Love Madge's signs," Father Teehan said.

I waved back. "Lots of people helped make those."

Reverend Jamison looked up from where he was laying out brochures about the pantry. "No kidding."

I headed to the end of the boardwalk, which has the kiddie rides and a large open space that usually holds picnic tables and lounge chairs. Today the tables were spread along the boardwalk and the open space was where we had scheduled Cinco de Mayo activities.

We had four piñatas that would be swatted at different times throughout the afternoon. Two were for groups of children from four to ten, and two for ages eleven to fifteen. I figured it would be a madhouse no matter how we divided the age groups.

Megan, Alicia, and Alicia's friend Clark were in charge of the piñatas. Max would help after he finished doing helium balloons with Harry, but I could tell from his nervous demeanor that he wasn't sure what to do.

I approached him. "I'm so glad you're here, Max."

"Helping with swatting. Swatting." His eyes darted to Alicia, then Megan, then me.

"Do you know what you're supposed to do?"

"No hitting. Make sure there is no hitting."

I realized this could be too little structure for Max. "Let's check with Megan."

She saw us coming and her eyebrows went up. She could tell I'd figured something was up with Max.

"Jolie, did Max tell you he's helping with the piñata today?"

"He did. I wondered if a good job would be passing the stick to each child as they get ready to swat?"

Megan grasped the issue at once. Max is so willing to help that sometimes we forget his role has to be somewhat narrow and clearly defined. She smiled. "That's a great idea. What do you think about that, Max?"

He smiled broadly. "I can pass the stick. Pass the stick."

Alicia had heard us and came over. "Come on Max. We give shorter kids longer sticks. I'll show you the sizes and help you pick.

Megan and I watched Max walk away. She shook her head. "How did I miss that?"

"You didn't miss anything. He probably just figured out he didn't know what to do, and I ran into him."

She nodded. "That man is so fortunate to have us."

I gave her a one-armed hug. "And the rest of us are lucky to have you."

She headed back to piñata set-up territory just as someone called to me.

I grinned at brightly dressed Harvest for All board member, Aretha, and two Spanish-language teachers from the middle school, also sporting what I think of as bright, Mexican dresses. They were to oversee small-group cha cha lessons. I smiled to myself. Aretha could organize an army. The lessons should go smoothly.

"You guys ready to jiggle?"

Aretha issued her deep laugh. "You tell that Scoobie husband I expect to see him over here shaking his tailbone."

The teachers, whose badges said Elena and Maria, didn't know me, and appeared unsure how I'd take the instruction about my husband's tailbone.

I grinned at the three of them. "You'll probably have to fight him off."

At noon I stood under a Harvest for All banner at one of the main entries to the boardwalk. Though I greeted various people as they arrived for the fundraiser, I also scoped the crowd for Scoobie and the twins. At twelve-twenty I saw them half-a-block from the boardwalk.

I walked down the steps to the street and grabbed the front of the stroller to help Scoobie heft it up the steps to the boardwalk. "How come you brought the side-by-side stroller?"

Leah piped up, "I like to sit next to my brother."

Oddly, Lance said nothing.

Scoobie stood behind the stroller so the kids couldn't see his expression or actions. He pointed down to Lance. "Somehow half a glass of orange juice found its way to one seat of the other stroller."

The kids like the wide stroller so they can talk to each other. Its width makes it hard to maneuver in a crowd. Scoobie says it comes in handy as a bulldozer.

I gave Scoobie an empathetic head shake. "We can take turns. I'll take them over to the salt water taffy place if you want to look around."

The twins love the taffy machine, which turns a huge line of taffy in a continual figure eight formation. They especially enjoy watching Mr. Fitzpatrick change the candy's colors. Fortunately they don't like to eat the sticky stuff.

We split up and Scoobie went to check out all of the booths. He had probably secured half of them. He's lived in Ocean Alley all his life and knows people from all walks of life. I've been here about six years, and most people I know are either through him and Aunt Madge, Harvest for All, or the appraisal business.

The twins entertained people with their squeals of delight for about twenty minutes as they watched the constantly moving taffy stretcher. By that time, I could tell Kevin had tired of waving at them from inside the store and I had had enough of watching the circulating taffy. I put them back into the stroller and we made our way toward the piñata game.

We had not gone far when a thin-faced man slowed his pace as he walked by us and glanced down at the twins. This happens many times a week, but there was something about his gaze that disturbed me. He lifted his eyes to mine and, without smiling, said, "Cute kids. I bet you keep a close eye on them."

I said nothing until he had passed me and then turned and in a loud voice said, "A very close eye."

I shut my eyes briefly to commit him to memory. His hair under a baseball cap looked black, and his skin had an olive tone. I guessed him to be about five-feet-eleven. His dark green corduroy sport jacket didn't go with either the temperature or the festive atmosphere.

Running footsteps came from behind me. "Jolie, slow down."

I turned to see Kevin panting slightly.

As he reached us he turned his head. "I think that was the guy! The guy from her driveway."

CHAPTER THIRTEEN

I STARED AT KEVIN. "Are you sure?"

Kevin's nod was emphatic. "I know it is!"

Leah said, "Hi Kevin."

Lance ignored Kevin in favor of trying to grab a poodle's tail. Fortunately, he missed.

"We have to call your uncle!"

"I'm going to follow him." Kevin turned and jogged in the direction of the man with the baseball cap.

I called after him, but Kevin didn't turn around. I pulled my phone from the pocket of my slacks and pushed the speed dial for Scoobie. He picked up, and I said, "We're in front of the souvenir shop a couple of doors down from the taffy place. I need you here."

He was with us in less than thirty seconds and I relayed where Kevin had gone and why. He nodded and began jogging down the boardwalk in the same direction.

I dialed Morehouse's cell phone. He answered as I turned the twins' stroller around to follow Scoobie. "I'm not sure if Kevin was correct, but he thinks he saw the man from Sandra's driveway. He went after him and now Scoobie is going after Kevin."

"You at your boardwalk thing?"

"Yes. They were going north from near the taffy place."

Before the twins and I had gone half a block I could hear the sirens. We reached one of the staircases that led down to the street, but I couldn't take the stroller down by myself. Besides, they might still be on the boardwalk, or have used another set of steps.

"We need grape popsicles," Lance announced.

I looked up and down the boardwalk. "We'll try to find some when Daddy gets back. You might have to settle for grape snow cones."

A police car pulled up on the street below, and Dana Johnson got out. She saw me and waved and came up the steps at a fast clip. "Have you seen them since you called Morehouse?"

"No. I don't know if they're together or whether…" I pointed. Scoobie and Kevin came toward us. Relief surged through me. I hadn't realized how tense I felt until my shoulders relaxed.

Leah clapped and Lance called, "We're getting grape popsicles, Daddy."

I listened as Scoobie and Kevin described walking several blocks down the boardwalk without seeing the man, and deciding to return to me. My impression was that Scoobie had made the decision for them. I was surprised not so much at Kevin's insistence that it was the man he had seen outside Sandra's house as that he wanted to follow him.

Dana jotted in a small notebook as she listened. When Kevin paused she asked, "I believe you are convinced, Kevin. But tell me why. You saw him briefly that night and it was dark. How can you be sure?"

Kevin glanced around. People had paused as they walked by, and then passed us. One of the guys from the track team grew closer. "What's up Kevin? Get your pocket picked?"

"Keep movin' Mahoney." Kevin looked again at Dana. "I saw him out the salt water taffy window. He looked at me in the place. He has this stare. It's like he's telling you to shut up with his eyes."

Dana raised her eyebrows. "That's interesting. You gave us a description earlier, but you didn't work with a sketch artist. If we brought one in do you think you could do that?"

Kevin shrugged as only a teenage boy can.

Morehouse's police-issued Caprice screeched to a halt. I turned to Dana. "The man spoke to me as he walked by the twins and me. I might be able to help with a sketch." I relayed his description.

Leah yelled, "We need to walk to the popsicles!"

As Morehouse came up the steps, Scoobie took the handles of the stroller. He looked at Dana. "You know what I know. I've got to take the twins down to the ice cream place. And Jolie has a bunch of stuff to do here."

I glanced at my watch. "Yikes it's almost time for the piñatas. I'm supposed to help keep the kids from swatting each other." I looked at Scoobie. "I'll follow you in two minutes."

Morehouse strode toward us, every inch of him looking as if he wanted to punch someone. He studied Kevin. "You okay?"

Kevin and Dana took turns saying what had happened. Then Dana nodded to me. "Jolie may have had the best look at the guy."

"I told Dana what he looks like, and later today or tomorrow I can come down to your office if you call me. But I need to get down to the other end of the boardwalk."

A less tense-looking Morehouse said, "I'm okay with that. I think Kevin and I will drive around to see if we can spot this guy."

"Good deal." I turned and walked rapidly toward the kiddie ride area. I felt relieved that Kevin would be with his uncle. I also wanted to find Terry to tell him what had happened. If the man actually was in the area, I didn't want him and Kevin looking for the guy. I wanted them at our house or Kevin's place.

Several people called to me and I waved or said hello, but I kept moving. I did stop briefly at the bake sale table and gave Aunt Madge a fifteen second summary of the last few minutes. "If you see Terry, tell him to find me."

She passed a cupcake to a teenage girl. "He's already at the piñata game."

I grinned at the button she sported. 'This is experience working.' People could ask her about it, but she wasn't being overtly political at a charity event.

A man called, "Afternoon, Jolie."

Jack Borman didn't stop. Instead, he moved through the crowd, introducing himself, and shaking hands. I caught snatches of what he said. "Beautiful accommodations. Indoor and outdoor pools."

"He thinks he's God's gift to Ocean Alley," I said.

Aunt Madge shrugged. "Except to me. He's gone by several times and doesn't say hello. I think I'm supposed to be insulted."

I grinned. "Lucky you."

I went to the ice cream window, where Scoobie was explaining to the twins that no popsicles were for sale today, only ice cream or snow cones. "You need help or do you want to catch up by the piñatas?"

He grinned. "We're good. I'm going to let them out of the stroller to eat and then walk down to find you."

I saw a man in a baseball cap, but it wasn't the thin-faced man. I drew a breath. *Stay smiling, stay in charge.* "Aretha says you have to do the cha-cha lessons."

His eyebrows went up and down. "Ooh la la."

I laughed and headed toward the first round of piñata swatting, already underway. Megan, Alicia, and Clark seemed to have the kids fairly well organized. Max proudly held several sticks, waiting to pass them to kids.

We had agreed that each child could have one minute to blindly swing the bat. Since this was a group of younger kids, I doubted any would have the strength to actually break the paper maché donkey.

We announced in advance that if no one broke the piñata, one of the adults would smash it and the kids could scramble for the goodies. Since the piñata's contents were of more interest than the swatting, at least for most kids, I figured it should go smoothly.

I glanced around for Terry. He must have gone from the piñata game area to another part of the boardwalk.

I allowed myself to take a breath and then grabbed a seat on the bench next to Sylvia Parrett, our longest-serving Harvest for All board member. A couple of years ago, a very proper Sylvia would have thought the event was either too loud or too messy. Today she looked as if she was having a great time. "How long have they been at this?"

"Hi Jolie. Close to ten minutes, I think. I saw you with the twins earlier."

"Scoobie has them. They're getting ice cream. I hope he has enough wipes."

Sylvia has been treasurer for almost four years. Sometimes her precision drives me crazy, but I wouldn't want the job.

"How much did we make in booth fees?" I asked.

"Some people paid more than the basic fee, as a donation. So almost $900. She nodded to herself. "Between the retail donations, raffles, and donations to play a couple of games, I bet we hit $10,000."

"I hope you're right." My eyes traveled throughout the crowd, continuing to search for the thin-faced man in the ball cap. What would have been his point in coming here? Was he trying to scare Kevin? It made no sense. Now more people knew what he looked like.

His remark about keeping an eye on the twins really bothered me. They are never more than a couple of feet from either of us, unless we're at the playground, which is fenced in. Still, if he had connected me to Kevin and wanted to frighten me, it worked.

A glance down the boardwalk revealed Scoobie pushing the stroller, following the twins who walked ahead of it. I tapped Sylvia on the shoulder. "I'm going to join Scoobie in corralling the kids."

She didn't take her eyes off the piñata swatting. "Good luck."

I walked toward them and stopped when I reached them. Lance held up his hands, palms toward me. "Grape hands."

"Do they taste good?"

He licked a palm and made a face. "No."

Leah seemed to be fading. "Push me Daddy."

He lifted her into the stroller and she put her head on its food tray.

Lance looked as if he was about to make a dash for the poodle we'd seen earlier. I picked him up. "Are you a tired boy?"

He yawned. "No, Mommy."

I patted him on the back and he rested his head on my shoulder. "Maybe you should take them you-know-where."

Scoobie shook his head. "George and Ramona can watch them for a couple minutes. I think I can win the cha cha contest."

CHAPTER FOURTEEN

BETWEEN THE FUNDRAISER AND the man who commented about keeping an eye on the twins, Saturday had been crazy. We needed some calm time.

Sunday morning, we trundled the twins to church. They like the toddler babysitting room, with its brightly colored walls and three boxes of toys. After the service, we had donuts and coffee with Madge and Harry. Since no jelly donuts were available, the twins stayed clean.

Reverend Jamison circulated and eventually made it to our table. He shook his head toward Scoobie. "Sorry you didn't win the cha cha contest."

Scoobie grinned. "Incentive for next year."

Jamison turned to Aunt Madge. "How are you holding up, Madge?"

"Even when I'm sad or mad," she gestured to the twins with her head, "I'm always fine."

Harry added, "And we're so busy with her campaign, we probably don't think of Sandra enough."

Jamison's gaze fell on me. "You pulled off another one, Jolie. Thanks so much."

"Scoobie got most of the vendors and community organization booths," I said. "Everybody pitched in."

Scoobie and I shared a look, and he said, "Jolie is so tired she thinks it's Tuesday, so we're good."

"Hey." I threw a wadded napkin at him.

"No throwing," Leah said.

Jamison stooped so he was eye-level with the twins in their booster seats. "Did you have fun on the boardwalk yesterday?"

"I burped grape snow cone," Lance said.

"I picked candy off the ground," Leah added. "From the paper donkey's bottom."

SCOOBIE TOOK THE KIDS to the food pantry to sort cans, and I headed for the grocery store. When I got back to the house, Terry and Kevin had made sandwiches and stationed themselves in front of the television. Any house feels small with two teenage boys parked in the middle of a room.

"Hi guys. A little R&R before Sunday afternoon homework.?"

Terry turned his head toward me. "Jolie. What did we say about embarrassing me in front of my friends?"

I laughed and so did they.

Kevin looked behind me. "Where are Scoobie and the twins?"

I sat my two sacks of groceries on a table.

"You have more to carry in?" Terry asked.

"No, thanks. They're at Harvest for All. Scoobie is helping sort some of the donations from this weekend. We have a little gated area for the kids."

"Aren't they kind of big for something like that?" Kevin asked.

"They could easily get out. There are hundreds of things that could fall from the shelves onto their heads, so the deal is if they play in there they get a Happy Meal later."

"Lucky kids," Kevin said, and turned back to the television.

I headed to the kitchen, put groceries away, and took a pound of hamburger from the back of the fridge. I planned to make spaghetti.

Kevin came into the kitchen as I turned on the stove to cook the meat. He sat at the table.

"Jolie, do you think that man will come back?"

I didn't want to give him a response meant only to be comforting. "My guess is he wanted you to see him so he'd know if you recognized him. Now he knows you do…"

"You think he'll come back?"

"It wouldn't make sense."

Kevin sat up straighter in his chair and leaned forward. "Why not? He could figure out where I hang out."

I talked fast so he didn't interrupt. "But at this point, he has to know that not only do you know who he is, but I do. We've described him to the police and they issued some vague 'person of interest' statement yesterday evening. I heard it on the car radio. If harm were to come to you, he'd be the first suspect."

"Huh." Kevin took an apple from the bowl on the table. "I guess that makes sense."

"So far, no one seems to recognize him from that description, I doubt he lives in Ocean Alley. He knows not to come back."

"I could see him somewhere else. He wouldn't like that."

I concentrated on breaking up the hamburger and using a spatula to turn it in the pan. "If he is some kind of criminal, he might change his appearance so you don't recognize him. Then you're no threat to him and he won't bother you."

He stood. "I bet he does, like, dye his hair or something."

Terry stuck his head in the doorway. "Let's go get ice cream."

Kevin left the kitchen and started toward the front door. Over his shoulder he called, "Thanks, Jolie."

I met Terry's gaze, and he mouthed "thank you" before he followed Kevin.

THE MONDAY PAPER ALWAYS has a huge article, complete with a photo spread, about any Harvest for All fundraiser. Everyone whose picture was in it, or knew someone with a picture, wants a copy. The paper prints extras.

I tried to look at some of the many shots while I cut up bananas for the twins to eat in the van. Scoobie and I had decided he should follow us to the daycare for a couple of days, to be sure no one was scoping us out, as he said.

The earliest drop-off was seven-thirty, so when Scoobie drove on to work, the twins and I would sit in the parking lot for thirty minutes. I had two wet washcloths in plastic bags plus clean shirts, in case the bananas ended up smeared on a twin. Or when they did.

As I was about to fold the paper shut, a color photo of one of Aunt Madge's signs drew my attention. "Oh, damn."

Scoobie walked in with Leah riding piggyback. "What?"

I pointed. "Did Aunt Madge put up the signs herself, or her volunteers?"

"Volunteers, I guess. Uh oh."

In the middle of the page was one of the off-message signs Scoobie had made. "Madge for Boss. Do What She Says."

AFTER DROPPING OFF THE TWINS at daycare, I drove to the Popsicle District to appraise a cottage that Lester had written a contract on for a ridiculously high price. He advertises occasionally in a neighborhood paper in New York City. There he finds wealthy people who have no idea about the true value of houses in Ocean Alley. He convinces them to make ludicrous offers for houses that Lester has listed too high.

I parked in front of the cornflower blue house and studied its exterior. New windows and gutters, plus an added sunroom on the right. They would help, but likely not enough.

Lester had given me the key to the front door. I traipsed onto a new front porch and let myself in. "Ooh.

Pretty wood floors. They must have had these refinished."

I shut the door and got to work. The current owner had left a few pieces of furniture so the house would show better. Since the rooms were not crowded, I had the three bedrooms and living room measured in fifteen minutes.

As I walked back through the living room toward the kitchen, movement on the front porch caught my eye. A face peered at me through glass panes on the door.

The thin-faced man had not changed his appearance.

I dropped my notebook and reached into my pocket for my phone as I turned to dash into a bedroom. I hoped those doors had locks.

In a loud voice, the man said, "It's not what you think!"

I stopped before entering the hallway to the bedroom and turned. The front door was locked. He couldn't get to me quickly. "What do you mean?"

He closed his eyes for a second and drew a breath. I sensed relief on his part.

"I was in her driveway the night the Cartwright woman was killed. But I didn't do it."

I stared at him. Would a guilty man track me down? *Sure, if he wanted to kill you.* "Why did you try to scare me when I had the twins on the boardwalk last Saturday? It sounded like a threat."

"It was a warning. But I'm not the threat. Look, can we talk? Indoors?"

151

I shook my head. "I'm not crazy. We can talk through the door. But I'm not coming any closer." I held up my phone. "It would only take a second to lock myself in a bedroom and call 9-1-1."

"I guess I see your point." He drew a breath. "You saw me before last Saturday, but only from the back."

I frowned. "I have a decent memory for faces."

He smiled fully. "My face is on my front. And my name is Peter Clayton, by the way."

The smile made him seem less threatening, friendly even. I studied his lightly lined face. Probably in his early forties. Black hair with little gray. Brown eyes. Maybe five-ten. "Where did I see you?"

"The day you went to Quentin Wharton's office to talk about something. When you left, a man was in his outer office, looking at a picture on the wall. That was me. Remember? I didn't turn fully around."

I considered what he said. My mind had been on Sandra, but also on the fundraiser. I had made the proverbial beeline for the door. A memory stirred.

"I don't remember what you looked like. But I remember why you were there."

He did a shoulder-height fist pump. "Yes! Insurance."

I smiled, still wary. "Okay. You know Wharton. Why does that make a difference?"

"It may help people understand that Quentin sent me to Sandra Cartwright's house to see if she was dead."

PETER CLAYTON SAT ON THE top porch step, facing the street, watching for a police car. I studied him from behind, but from a couple feet back from the door.

He certainly looked like Mr. Average. Blue collared shirt, top button undone, and a loose-knotted tie.

I assumed the car in front of the house was his. He didn't look like a Volkswagen kind of guy, but I supposed it got good gas mileage. Bright red, though. I thought that was a color involved in a lot accidents. You'd think an insurance agent would know that.

Dana Johnson parked her squad car in front of the cornflower blue house and she and Corporal Blaine got out. I unlocked the door and joined Clayton, who stood from his position on the top porch step.

Dana took him in, stopped, and glanced at me.

I nodded. "Yes, he matches the description. But I think he has something important to tell you, and I believe him when he says he didn't kill Sandra."

Clayton stood and held out a hand as he walked down the steps. "Peter Clayton. I live between here and Lakewood, and sell the hospital its liability insurance."

"Dana Johnson." She stepped forward and shook his hand.

Corporal Blaine did the same. "Might be easier if we talked at the station."

Clayton nodded. "I'm fine with that. I just wanted to remind Jolie here that she'd seen me at the hospital one day."

Dana's eyebrows shot up in my direction.

I shrugged. "Only from the back."

MOREHOUSE SAT IN THE CONFERENCE room to participate in the conversation with Peter Clayton. He shot eye daggers at me. I shrugged at him. Sergeant

Morehouse had been mad at me plenty of times. He gets over it.

As Dana introduced Clayton to Captain Tortino, I leaned toward Morehouse and spoke quietly. "You can be on the investigation again?"

"Wasn't Kevin's skin under Sandra's fingernails."

"DNA?" I whispered.

He gave me a withering look. "No scratch marks on my nephew."

Clayton nodded at Sergeants Morehouse as he and Dana Johnson sat at the table. Tortino stood in the doorway, and Clayton glanced at him, too. "I appreciate you talking to me without trying to lock me up first."

Dana nodded. "So, you were in Sandra Cartwright's driveway the night she was killed, and you believe you are the person Kevin Falcon saw as he stood on the porch?"

He took a breath. "I know I was. I had just gone out her back door and come around the house, heading for the street. I parked a few houses down from hers."

"And why did you enter her house?" Dana asked.

"I had a call from Quentin Wharton. He said she had fallen and he wanted me to check on her."

"Did he say why he thought she mighta had something needed checked?" Morehouse asked.

Clayton cleared his throat. "He said he had been told she tripped and maybe hit her head on the edge of the fireplace."

"You mean the lip?" I asked.

Tortino shook his head slightly in my direction. I sat back in my chair.

"Yeah," Clayton said, "the raised edge around the fireplace. I told him he worked at the hospital, why didn't he check? Then I figured he was either there when she fell, or somebody else called him. Either way, he didn't want to check on her."

"So you went there," Dana stated.

"I did. I don't know a lot about bodies, but I was with my mother when she died. The nurse, Sandra, was...she had no pulse."

"And you're sure Wharton never told you how he knew Ms. Cartwright had been seriously injured?" Dana asked.

Clayton nodded.

Morehouse had his look of skepticism. I've seen it often. "Why didn't you call the police?"

"I didn't want to call from inside her house. I figured, I guess it was cowardly, I'd call from my car. Block the caller ID. But then the kid saw me."

"And you took off. Just left it at that," Dana said.

"I did, but I looked back, saw the kid had gone into the house. Figured he would call 9-1-1 or something."

Tortino finally asked the question I wanted to. "Why would Quentin Wharton call you?"

Clayton sighed. "I'd met with him after work, and was supposed to meet with him again in the morning. He knew I was staying overnight at Beachcomber's Alley to work up some revised estimates."

"Meet about what?" Dana asked.

"The hospital buying more liability insurance. Wharton wanted estimates if they had to expand hours in the ER, do other things if the developer started building that big resort."

"That don't explain why he called you," Morehouse said.

Clayton frowned in his direction. "He knew I wanted the money from that commission, so I'd pretty much do what he asked."

Tortino moved away from the doorway, back to captain duties, I assumed.

"So," Morehouse said, "now you decided that instead of callin' us, you'd call a real estate appraiser?"

"He knew I saw…" I began.

More dagger eyes from Morehouse. "I'm askin' him, Jolie."

I nodded, feeling impatient. If they would just stop asking questions and let Clayton talk, it would go faster.

"She's right," Clayton said.

I kept myself from giving Morehouse a sarcastic wave.

"I was in Wharton's outer office one day when she came out of some meeting with him. Jolie only saw my back, but I thought she might remember I'd been there if I reminded her."

Morehouse turned his gaze to me. "And did you?"

"Not his face, but the topic I heard him start to talk to Wharton about."

"Insurance," Clayton and I both said.

Dana pointed a pencil at Clayton. "Let's say we believe you, and go talk to Quentin Wharton. If he were careful, there could be no clear evidence that he called you. Can you offer any support for the call to you?"

"I…don't know. He called me at the hotel."

"Great," Morehouse said. "If he called from a phone other than his, we might get a record of a call to the main number at about the time you'll tell us, but not who called or that the call was transferred to you."

"Maybe the hotel operator will remember Wharton called," I volunteered.

Morehouse stood. "Let me walk you out, Jolie."

I stood, nodded to Dana, and hesitated before I spoke to Clayton. "Good luck."

Morehouse led me out of the room, through the bullpen, and into the public area. I expected him to close the door behind me and return, but he came into the outer area with me.

He ran a hand over his cropped hair. "You tellin' him good luck, that might not be best right now."

"You think he's lying?"

"Don't matter what I think. What anyone thinks. Maybe he killed her, maybe he didn't. But we gotta have evidence before we get all kissy face with a guy coulda murdered Sandra."

"Good advice." I grinned. "Can I come back for the kissy face?"

He jerked his thumb toward the entrance. "You think of somethin' we need to know, call me."

I FELT AMAZINGLY LIGHT, in mood and spirit. Sandra was still dead, of course, but Terry's best friend was home and no one thought he had killed her. Now that I'd met the so-called thin-faced man, I also thought it unlikely he was a threat. Now, if we could just figure out who started the fire by Aunt Madge's garage.

I sat on a bench outside the police station and sent Scoobie a long text about my morning.

His replied with five exclamation points. His day never left much time for conversations, but at least he was saying he knew I'd had an eventful time thus far.

As I walked to my car, I thought about what Peter Clayton had said. Wharton told him "he had heard" Sandra might be hurt. Or something like that. He had to have heard that from someone, unless he did it.

Could Wharton have killed her? A member of the Endowment Committee who wanted her to change her thinking? Why would anyone care enough about helping the resort? Probably not someone who went there to kill her, someone who surprised her.

I discounted the burglar theory. Someone took her purse and jewelry to make it look like a robbery or burglary.

I wanted to talk about the situation with someone.

My first inclination was to call Scoobie, but he's always with other people, often patients. And he wouldn't ruminate with me. That left George, Lester or, in a pinch, Ramona. She would listen, but she wouldn't offer too many ideas, and she'd tell me to mind my own business.

I opted for George. He answered with an abrupt, "What's up, Jolie?"

"If you don't have time, you can call me later, okay?"

"I'll do that. Early afternoon okay?"

"Sounds good." I hung up.

Lester's office would be a better place to talk than Java Jolt, or even on the phone. Who knew where he'd be when he picked up? He'd holler my name and talk about Sandra or whatever in a bellow.

For the second time in a few days, I trudged up the exterior steps to Lester's second-floor office. I noted that the plastic fish that were spaced on the wall along the stairs had turned to a sort of lemon-green shade. Probably one of the buildings Wharton was referring to when he said Ocean Alley had a faded glory look.

I let myself into the hallway and walked down the narrow hallway toward Lester's office. He isn't supposed to smoke in the building, and if accused he always says he had his cigar lit right before he came into his office. Not likely. I knocked on the door frame.

Lester had the *Ocean Alley Press* spread across his desk, and quickly closed it. "Just catchin' up on house prices…Oh, hey Jolie. News?"

I grinned. "Lots of good articles on real estate in the sports section."

"Smart ass." He gestured to a chair across from his desk. "Toss those files on the floor and have a seat."

"I'll finish the measurements on that overpriced house in the Popsicle District this afternoon."

Lester pointed an index finger at me across the desk. "Hey. Plenty of houses cost that much in Ocean Grove or Bradley Beach." He stopped. "You know something."

"Kevin's off the hook for Sandra's murder, but I don't think the police know for sure who the killer was."

He sat back in his chair. "That'll be a load off for ol' Morehouse."

"Have you heard anything about people who didn't like Sandra?"

He shrugged. "Does it matter? You got kids and a job. Why care about that stuff now Terry's friend's in the clear?"

"I also have a husband."

"Goes with the kids. So?"

"At this point, I'm mostly concerned, I suppose."

"Guy on the boardwalk spook you?"

He did, but not anymore. "I figure he can't be that dangerous, or he wouldn't walk around at a public fundraiser on the boardwalk." I decided Lester hadn't heard anything about resort plans or anything that would tie to Sandra's death. I was starting to wonder why I cared.

"Guess your Aunt Madge is still pretty torn up about losing her friend."

That's why I care!! I couldn't believe I hadn't considered whether someone angry at Sandra would be equally furious with Aunt Madge.

"She is. The funeral was hard for her."

Lester stared at me. "You're thinkin' about something."

"Just that...I wish we knew who killed Sandra and why."

Lester glanced towards his newspaper. "We all wanna know. Good lady."

"Yes. I hope it's not about her opposition to the resort. She and Aunt Madge were both pretty vocal about it."

Lester sat back in his chair, which emitted a protesting squeak. "You don't got enough to do? Or maybe lack of sleep makes your mind wander."

I laughed. "I guess it does sound odd. I sleep okay."
I rose.

Lester stood, hands in his trouser pockets, jingling change. "I'm no official detective, but I think Madge would be a lousy target, especially for someone tied to the resort. Whole town would rise up against the place."

I hoped he was right.

CHAPTER FIFTEEN

GEORGE SHOWED MORE INTEREST in Peter Clayton's story. Admittedly, Lester would have had more to say if I'd actually mentioned Clayton, especially since the guy showed up at Lester's listing. But he would have blabbed to the town and Morehouse would have encouraged officers to give me tickets or something.

George and I sat in Java Jolt, and he ordered iced tea. "My inclination is to believe the guy, but either he's hiding who he thinks killed Sandra or he can only guess."

I mopped some of my iced tea off the table. "He may not know, but Wharton does."

"According to this Peter guy."

I nodded. "Just seems so risky for him to come forward to tell lies. Aside from his own reputation to protect, I can't imagine the hospital would buy any insurance from him again."

George shrugged. "Bottom line, Kevin is safe and the cops have more to look into."

"What about…what about Aunt Madge? If someone went after Sandra because she opposed them…"

George tapped a pen on the table. "Whoa. Are you bored or something? Someone could be really mad at her, but to go after her because she's mouthing off…"

He caught my raised eyebrows.

"Because she's raising important policy issues, would be nuts. Look, Madge has some strong arguments, but who does she really hurt by advocating against the resort? Or for small businesses for that matter. People are passionate on both sides."

"But she knows everyone," I insisted.

George smiled. "In your world. Ocean Alley has changed just in the last ten years. Lots of newer residents, there's even talk about needing another elementary school."

I gave him a grudging smile. "So, people won't vote for her just because she's volunteered for half the organizations in town at one time or another?"

"She's articulate, but Madge is no threat to resort developers or supporters. I doubt they're trying to figure out which candidates to bump off."

I laughed. "Okay. That takes me back to Peter Clayton. Wharton called him, but he may not be who killed Sandra. Or he could be."

"Leave it to the police."

I thought I might. Kevin was not in danger from the man who saw him at Sandra's house, since that man was Clayton and he admitted it. If Kevin was safe, so was Terry. Harry was with Aunt Madge and they were pretty much always in public places."

"Okay. I'm not going to think about all this anymore."

FED TWINS WERE HAPPY TWINS, so I pulled already sliced carrots from the fridge as soon as we got home Monday afternoon. "Who wants a story before I go to Aunt Madge's to make tea?"

"Did they have Elmo when you were little?" Leah asked.

Lance slurped his apple juice. "When does Daddy get home?"

My kids love me to pieces, especially in the winter when they can't go outside to play and Jazz hides well. But I am no competition for Daddy.

Scoobie called at three. "Can you take the twins to Madge's? I'll get them before the guests come in for tea."

"Sure, I…"

"Great." Scoobie hung up.

Each twin stared at me from their respective spots on our kitchen floor. I honestly think they eat snacks on the floor to tempt Jazz to come close enough for a pat.

"Today is your lucky day. You get to come to Aunt Madge and Uncle Harry's house while the dogs and I get ready to serve tea and bread."

"Can Jazz come?" Leah asked.

I reached for her empty sippy cup and sat it on the kitchen table. "Today's kind of busy. Maybe another day."

"What if she got out the door?" Lance asked.

I stared down at him, hands on hips. "She could get hit by a car."

Lance scrambled to his feet. "Jazz should stay home."

I debated hauling out the stroller from the back deck, but that would take too long. Of course, walking to the house next door could take longer, but I'd risk it.

In twenty minutes, Leah and Lance were settled in front of the sliding glass doors in the great room, one dog by each twin. They held their respective favorite stuffed animals and stared out the door looking for chipmunks or baby bunnies. If my hands hadn't been covered in flour I'd have taken a photo.

With tea water boiling in the kettle and bread in the oven, I sat on the floor next to them. "Do you want your crayons and drawing paper so you can make something for Aunt Madge and Uncle Harry?"

Lance glanced at me. "Did you see her bottom drawer?"

"In her bedroom," Leah added.

"Did you guys snoop in their bedroom?"

They shook their heads. Leah added, "She saves all our pictures."

"In the drawer," Lance said.

"And she showed you?" I asked.

"She showed Daddy," Lance said.

Leah giggled. "We peeked."

SCOOBIE ARRIVED AT TEN before four o'clock. As soon as he walked into the great room the twins launched themselves at him.

"What are my favorite chuckleheads doing?" he demanded.

"Coloring," Leah said.

Lance tossed a whiffle ball in the dogs' direction. "For everybody."

Scoobie glanced at me. "A lot going on."

I nodded toward the guest breakfast room. "I figured. But I have to get the bread out there."

"I'll take the twins out for a walk with the dogs, and we'll come back here in forty-five minutes or so."

He hadn't finished the sentence when the two retrievers stood and shook their fur with vigor.

"I'll be here."

As I carried the second loaf of bread into the great room, Bart Mobley came in. He shuffled to the credenza and poured himself tea. "I heard the police are talking to Sandra Cartwright's boss. Or some bigwig at the hospital, anyway."

I offered him jam. "Aren't you Mr. Well-Informed."

"I'm not, but my cousin is. The one who dated Sandra. He's been talking to everybody he knows every day."

The other two guests had finished their tea and wanted to take a couple of pieces of bread up to their room. I wrapped them in foil and offered butter, which they refused. Aunt Madge's recipes really need no condiments.

I put my elbows on Bart's table and rested my chin on my fists. "So, what did you hear?"

"Police went by the hospital, oh, maybe one o'clock or so. My cousin said his friend who works in the blood lab said they're asking people if they remember anything from the last couple days Sandra worked." He dipped bread in his tea and dripped it on the table. "My cousin, Henry's his name, said they spent the most time with that Wharton fellow."

Translation: Bart heard mostly rumors.

I stood. "I'll feel better when they arrest someone."

"You think I should stay in town until they do? On account of all this is hard on Henry."

Such a lonely guy. "Aunt Madge isn't fully booked right now, not until after Memorial Day. You're welcome to stay for a few more days. Not sure she'll have room election night."

He headed for the television in the guests' living room and I cleared the tables and wrapped up leftover bread. I'd take some and leave some for Madge and Harry.

I had just finished loading the dishwasher when Scoobie, twins, and dogs came in the sliding glass doors.

Lance practically danced across the room. "We saw birds building a nest!"

Leah held out a dandelion. "And we picked you a flower."

I stooped to give them both hugs. "I'm such a lucky Mommy."

Scoobie had unhooked the dogs' leashes and they slopped water from their bowls. He reached down and pulled me up. "Hello Domestic Goddess."

"You always say that," Leah said. They walked back to their coloring books.

Scoobie grinned and we sat at Madge and Harry's oak table. "What do you know? Or better yet, what kept you late?" I asked.

"More what I think I know. Gina who works with me is friends with Marleen in Wharton's office. The police were with him for forty-five minutes, much longer than the day they found Sandra. When they left, Wharton shut the door to his office and didn't come out."

"But if they didn't take him with them, what's the big deal?"

Scoobie shrugged. "I think it's more that people think he's nervous. If they told him what your thin man buddy said, he should be damn nervous."

"Is he so unpopular that people enjoy seeing him sweat?"

"Apparently he was a lot nicer boss before he started working more with the board."

"And did you have late patients?" I asked.

"The police came down to talk to Sam. Usually two of us are available, so I stayed over to be sure Gina wasn't working alone."

Sam has always been vocal about needing more staff or equipment, but I didn't think he'd been especially close to Sandra. "Just general questions for him, you think?"

"He'd talked to Sandra several times lately about using some endowment funds to replace our open MRI machine. It's more than ten years old."

I did an exaggerated shrug.

Scoobie mimicked it back to me. "Sam didn't say anything when Dana left."

"Oh, Dana talked to him? That's good."

He nodded. "I think it's just that he was on her schedule a few times. If he had seen anything odd, I'm sure he would have already told them."

MOREHOUSE CALLED AFTER THE twins had been in bed for an hour and Terry had just finished writing a take-home exam question. "Jolie. I shoulda asked you not to talk to anyone but Scoobie about this morning."

"Well…I said something to George, but I don't think he'll blab."

"Crud."

Morehouse spoke so loudly that Scoobie looked up from his book and grinned. I put Morehouse on speaker phone.

"I can call him and ask him not to…"

"I will."

Before Morehouse hung up, I asked, "Did you figure out anything?"

After two beats of silence, he said, "From the way Wharton talked, you'd think he barely knew your buddy Peter Clayton."

Scoobie mouthed "your buddy."

I half-snorted. "He knew him well enough to ask him to go check out a body!"

"Accordin' to Clayton. But like I told you, it may be hard to prove anything. For a few days at least. So, keep a lid on it." He hung up.

I looked at the phone and then Scoobie. "He's so infuriating."

Scoobie went back to his book. "The feeling's always been mutual, I think."

I glanced at Terry on the other side of our long living room. The phone seemed attached to his head, as it had been a lot the last couple of days. Probably he and Kevin had a lot to catch up on.

I SPENT MUCH OF TUESDAY morning at Harvest for All, in the basement of First Prez. Scoobie, Alicia, her friend Clark, and our board member Aretha had sorted the nearly two thousand cans that came in Saturday. Hardly any were out of date, and very few were cans of sauerkraut or cranberry jelly.

The Cotton Candy Shoppe collected the most cans, in part because they gave away the sticky treat to everyone who gave them a can. We were fortunate they won handily (an election landslide, George called it), because can counting is not precise when you're dealing with dozens of donor stores and booths.

The food pantry is only about forty feet by forty feet, with shelves situated behind a counter. With little storage space, I had to decide where to put all the donations.

Mr. Markle had given us lots of empty boxes. We usually don't have to store a lot, because when we get donations in the fall and early winter, we give it away really quickly for Thanksgiving and Christmas.

I called Megan at Java Jolt to pick her brain. "Hmm. We don't want to move heavy boxes around town. Why don't you see if we can use the big closet under the staircase that goes upstairs? I think it's empty because some water leaked in last year."

"Oh, right. But the leak was fixed." I walked up the steps to get the closet key from Reverend Jamison's secretary. She didn't used to think I was holy enough to run the pantry, but I'd grown on her. She gave me the key and told me where to find a dolly.

In the BT era, moving heavy boxes was something I left to Scoobie – or anyone else, unless I had no choice. Now that I schlepp a twin on each hip, I'm much stronger.

The Sunday can sorters had organized food by fruit, vegetables, soup, meat, and boxed meals or rice. The latter I wouldn't put in a closet. No sense tempting mice. I had ten boxes moved when my cell phone chirped.

In a very friendly tone, Quentin Wharton said, "Jolie, why don't you stop by?"

I debated telling Morehouse about the call. No one had officially said Wharton killed Sandra. The man had every right to call me. And Scoobie did work there. Would I refuse to talk to his CEO?

If I called Morehouse, he'd tell me to butt out. Besides, maybe I'd learn something that would indicate whether Wharton called Peter Clayton to protect himself or someone else.

CHAPTER SIXTEEN

IT SEEMED I HAD BECOME Quentin Wharton's buddy. At least someone he wanted to ruminate with. He actually asked Marleen to get us coffee. Instead of sitting across from his desk, he invited me to take a seat in the grouping of overstuffed chairs in a corner of his office.

"So, Jolie. Did the fundraiser go well?"

You needed to talk to me about that? "Very well. Thanks for participating. The boardwalk businesses seemed to like it so much we may make it an annual event."

His nod was solemn. "Nutrition is so important for children. For anyone."

"Yes. Fortunately we have a lot of volunteers who think so, too."

"We tried to keep track of how many visited our booth. I'd say more than 200 people, not counting little kids."

"Did, uh, more of your board members come by?"

"Several, and Jack Borman sat with us for a time. I know he isn't your aunt's favorite person, but he's shown a lot of interest in the hospital."

"Ah. George and I talked to him in his office, briefly, on Friday."

Wharton began to take apart a paperclip. "What did you think of him?"

"He's certainly focused on getting the resort built."

Wharton continued to concentrate on his paperclip. "He plans to get involved in the community. But…"

Apparently I was supposed to ask him to continue. "But what?"

"He lets me know what he thinks of people. I've never been a fan of talking about people behind their backs."

Until now? "He must love Aunt Madge."

Wharton smiled briefly. "Much as you would expect."

I wasn't sure where the conversation was going. Was he trying to put distance between himself and Borman? Why would he think I cared? "Do you believe the resort, if it goes through, will contribute to the hospital?"

He nodded forcefully. "I'm so sure of it, I thought about talking to Borman about joining his team."

I frowned. "You mean leave the hospital?"

He half-shrugged. "I haven't always worked in health care. A good manager can run anything. But I decided not to pursue it."

Why is he telling me this?

I said nothing, so Wharton added, "Borman will bring a lot of business, a lot of jobs to Ocean Alley, but his attitude of 'anything to get the job done' is too intense for me. I've decided to stay right here."

If you won't be in jail. Is he trying to make me see Borman as a bad guy?

"I'm sure that will help the hospital if it does have to expand."

After two more minutes of innocuous conversation, I decided to ask a question that mattered, perhaps to see if he would reveal how angry he'd been with Sandra. "What did you think of Sandra's decision to resign?"

His eyes widened, but he covered his surprise quickly. "What makes you think that?"

"Gee, I heard it a couple of places. Something about the hospital endowment changing its investment strategy. Maybe with encouragement from the hospital board."

His face reddened slightly. "Rumors, that's all. People make up things."

"Actually, I'm fibbing a bit. When Lester and I went to assess her house's value, for her nephew, I saw a copy of her letter."

His expression, generally an animated one, froze for a moment. "A copy? There was a copy?"

I wanted to say I thought he hadn't known of her plans. Instead, I shrugged. "I assume the police found it.

I'm surprised they didn't mention it." *Since it could be a reason for an argument.*

He leaned back in his chair, and smiled. "Sandra may have thought about it. But she never turned in a letter. I don't think she could have left the hospital over something like hospital investments. All she cared about were the patients and her nurses."

I frowned. "Maybe someone wanted her to stop opposing the resort."

He shook his head firmly. "There's no evidence her death had a thing to do with any of these local...controversies. Someone broke in and she surprised them."

"You're probably right. Almost the saddest part is that if anyone had called an ambulance, the brain injury might not have killed her."

He flushed and spoke harshly. "Many people have said that. I understand that police sergeant's nephew was one of those at the scene."

One of them? He's saying he knew someone else went. "He was too late."

"How could a kid be sure? If he'd called for help instead of leaving..." He spread his hands in front of him, palms up.

I wondered what he knew about Clayton, if anything. "Sixteen-year-olds get scared. I think the man Kevin saw near her porch contributed to that as much as finding Sandra dead."

"So you don't think he made that up?"

Aha. He had been told Kevin saw someone. Who told him that?

I frowned. "Of course not. More important, the police believe what Kevin said."

His smile was tight-lipped. "They would, wouldn't they? He's kind of one of their own."

I glanced at my watch and stood. "Thanks for the invite. It's been good getting to know you better."

For some reason, Wharton didn't return my brilliant smile.

I REFLECTED ON THE conversation a lot. On the one hand, Wharton bad-mouthed Borman. On the other, he had considered working for the man.

Did Wharton want me to think Sandra and the hospital weren't sufficiently important to make him angry enough to kill? And why talk to me about any of it?

I had turned the conversation to Sandra to see if he had an opinion about her death. He seemed to know that Clayton had talked to me and the police. Did he know what Clayton had said?

Or was Clayton's appearance on the porch this morning something he and Wharton planned together? Perhaps as a way to cast suspicion on someone else. Or maybe Wharton had never called Clayton, perhaps someone else had and Clayton was trying to implicate Wharton.

My brain buzzed. This was life, not a TV show.

Then I had a moment of clarity. Sandra had scratched someone. Could scratches heal in nine days? The police would need a warrant to look for her purse and jewelry, but what about checking someone's arm for scratches?

If the police had the skin under Sandra's fingers, they needed DNA from a suspect. That kind of analysis took time. Plus, didn't the police or whomever need a suspect's permission to secure DNA directly from a suspect? What killer would readily grant that?

SCOOBIE DID NOT LIKE the way my day had progressed. We rarely disagree, but we didn't need to talk much to know an argument was brewing. We made an unspoken agreement not to discuss the day until even Terry was asleep.

We sat on the couch together, but a foot or so farther apart than usual.

Scoobie started. "What business did you have talking to Wharton?"

"He called. If I didn't go, don't you think it would have seemed suspicious?"

"Suspicious to whom, Jolie? Kevin is safe. You aren't in the middle of solving Sandra's murder."

"I didn't invite Peter Clayton to look for Kevin and me on the boardwalk Saturday, or find me at the house I was appraising."

"But after he told you and the police that Wharton called him to go over to Sandra's, you went to talk to Wharton."

I felt my face redden. "He called me to his office. In a public building. Not a...a warehouse on some New Jersey dock."

For a moment I thought Scoobie would laugh, but he didn't.

Scoobie closed his eyes and opened them a moment later. "No one really knows who the bad guys are here. Or who started that fire at Madge's garage."

I bristled. "Let's not throw that into this conversation. If Sandra's death was deliberate or an accident, an argument was probably over her opposition to using those endowment funds. That has nothing to do with the election."

"That's your assumption. Jolie, you're a mom with kids to take care of. You have to stay away from those people."

I swallowed and gave in. More or less. "I will not seek out anyone connected to this. If even Morehouse calls me, I'll let you know. Okay?"

I smirked and held out a hand to shake his. Scoobie pulled me to him in a hug. "You also have a husband, you know."

I smiled into his shoulder. "And I kind of like him."

I HALF-EXPECTED TO PICK up the Wednesday *Ocean Alley Press* and read a story about someone, heaven only knew who, being arrested for Sandra Cartwright's murder. Instead there was a brief update saying the police had found another witness who was "in the vicinity" of her residence the night Sandra died.

As I sat in the appraisal office Wednesday morning, George called. "Your husband is my best friend."

"I know that."

"And he has asked me not to encourage you in any further endeavors related to the murder or somebody trying to run over Kevin."

"That's just ducky."

George laughed. "He did not ask me not to share with you what I pick up."

I sat up straight and put my coffee mug on the table. "Do tell."

"Peter Clayton has an independent insurance agency, a small one that specializes in insurance for businesses. According to my talks with other companies I investigate for, it's not too big. He doesn't seem to mingle well, which you have to do to get clients."

"Hmm. I remember him saying Wharton called him to check on Sandra because Wharton knew Clayton wanted more business from the hospital."

"According to Clayton."

"I just said that."

George grunted. "Aren't we snarky."

"There's still the business of her purse and jewelry. Somebody has those."

"They're in a landfill somewhere by now," George said.

"So, what else did you find out?"

"Dr. Welby told you he thought the hospital Endowment Committee would not vote to invest in the resort. Mr. Greentree, the banker, believes they will and they're voting again later in the week."

I spoke slowly. "If that's true, Sandra's death most benefits Borman."

"Yep. And he could easily know Clayton, too."

"Are you going to talk to him?"

George snorted. "I think the odds of Jack Borman talking to me are pretty slim. I'm going to keep sniffing around Clayton, maybe a little around Wharton."

"Can't you tell Borman you want one more interview for that feature on the resort that you're writing for the paper?"

"Maybe later. What are you going to do?"

"For this, nothing. Let you pick my brain if you want."

"Slim pickings." George hung up.

I DEBATED CALLING DR. WELBY, but decided against it. He confirmed what I knew about past Endowment Committee business, but I doubted he would discuss upcoming votes.

Instead, I went to the library to look up more on Jack Borman. The Internet is great, but if I wanted to look at local business journals or a lot of news articles, I would need the library's hard copies or digital subscriptions.

Daphne waved at me as I walked to the computers. The first search, by his name and Shoreline Investments, brought up too many options. I narrowed it to New Jersey and still had a lot, but a more manageable number.

Jack Borman had built smaller projects in several Jersey shore towns and a couple much larger ones in Ocean City, Maryland. "Wow, look how huge those condo complexes are." Exactly what I didn't want to see in Ocean Alley.

He had received awards from local groups for things like "increasing the vitality of a community" or bringing jobs to a town. He had also been sued for beginning a project in a south Jersey community. He pled victim to the recession and eventually paid for some of the demolition of a partially finished hotel.

It sounded as if he backed out or cut back on developments when he couldn't get financing. Any builder would do that. Generally, though, they had a sense of what the financial picture was before they broke ground.

I exited the search program. I bet Jack Borman only had financing for his Ocean Alley project if he could get a bunch of local groups to essentially lend him money. If he backed out partway through, how many local entities could lose chunks of funds?

Peter Clayton popped into my head and I went back to the search program. I found only ads for his independent insurance agency, which gave "prompt personal service." Maybe because he didn't have a lot of clients.

SCOOBIE CALLED ABOUT NOON. "The police asked Wharton to come down to the station. He drove his own car, but they escorted him."

"Huh. I guess if you're a bigwig you don't get cuffed at work."

"Not sure it was an arrest, but definitely more than the conversation they had in his office after the police found that Clayton guy."

I decided not to comment on who found the man. Plus, he found me. "George called today."

"That's not usually news, is it?"

In a serious tone, I said, "He is obeying your order to keep me out of investigating."

"Jeez, Jolie. I'm not trying to run your life. I guess I want to protect you."

"I'm behaving. Just letting you know George is, too." *Pretty much.*

I HAD A PILE OF AUNT MADGE'S campaign flyers to pass out. Why not do it in Quentin Wharton's neighborhood? He lived near the Victorian with the three kitchens, in a house that had never been subdivided. I parked a block away and began walking.

Few people were home, and Aunt Madge's edict was that we leave the flyer and not knock on doors. Unlike houses in parts of towns with a lot of rental properties, every house on this block had flowers in full bloom. To accommodate the soil's mix of topsoil and sand, most were in pots.

I decided not to walk onto Wharton's porch. Instead I studied his place from in front of the houses across the street. Was Wharton married? How did I not know that?

My phone did another Internet search. Divorced. Big house for one person.

The street suddenly filled with the sounds of two cars with large engines. *Nuts.* Ocean Alley Police cars. They stopped in front of Quentin Wharton's house, and two people climbed out of each cruiser. Dana and Blaine were in one, and I didn't know the officers in the other car.

With no way to sink into the sidewalk, I called to Dana.

She said something quietly to Corporal Blaine and walked over to me. "What are you doing here, Jolie?"

I held up the stack of campaign flyers. "Election's getting close."

She placed one hand on a hip. "And you just happened to be on Quentin Wharton's street?"

I pointed to the block behind me. "I started down there. Had no idea where he lived."

Dana and I are close in age, though she and her husband have no children. She can usually see right through me. She turned. "Have at it."

She had only gone a couple feet when I said, "As long as you're here, what are you up to?"

She faced me again. "Looking for anything Quentin Wharton shouldn't have. And you didn't hear that from me."

I continued down the street, with no intention of crossing to Wharton's side of the road. Less than five minutes later, Dana and Blaine came out. He carried what I assumed was an evidence bag with a shape that looked almost one foot square. Could it be Sandra's purse?

The two officers drove away, but the other two stayed. Even if they found a pot of body parts taken from the hospital morgue, they wouldn't tell me. I turned toward my car. I'd never find out what was in that bag. And then I thought of George.

LESS THAN TWENTY MINUTES after I called him, George called back. "Wharton gave them carte blanche to search his house. Said they didn't need a search warrant. They got one anyway."

"Do you know what was in the bag Dana and that Blaine guy carried out?"

"No, but among the list of things they were looking for were her purse, the kinds of stuff usually in a woman's purse, including her wallet, and assorted jewelry. The only jewelry mentioned by name was a necklace with a cross."

"How do you know all those specifics?"

"In the warrant. Wasn't sealed. I'm going to assume they found some of what they were looking for."

I had pulled into the courthouse parking lot to answer George's call. "Weird that he kept it."

"I thought so, too."

Neither of us spoke for several seconds. I turned off my car engine. "Maybe someone planted it."

"Just like TV." George hung up.

I was going to the registrar of deeds' office, but maybe I could find out more about what was happening with Wharton. The police station wasn't attached to the courthouse and I had a reason to be in the building. No one could accuse me of snooping.

For the next hour I took more time than usual finding houses that were similar to those I was appraising. I visited the restroom once and the water fountain three times.

I walked into the clerk of court's office to say hello and asked about one of the staff who had recently had a baby. Eventually the clock edged toward three and I packed my briefcase.

As I left the registrar of deeds' office, Corporal Blaine almost mowed me down. "Sorry, Jolie."

To his back, I called, "Hope you found what you wanted."

Without looking back, he walked rapidly toward the elevator that led to various judges' chambers. "Sure did."

AFTER SUPPER, SCOOBIE HEADED to his Wednesday AA meeting with George and Terry helped me get the twins into the bathtub. Sometimes we skip, but today Lance had smeared ketchup on the inside of both arms. I didn't bother to ask why.

Lance and Leah said almost nothing.

"Why are you guys so quiet?"

Leah scrunched her nose. "Mommy, are you mad at Daddy?"

"No, I'm almost never mad at Daddy."

"Is Daddy mad at you?" Lance asked.

"You'd have to ask him to be sure, but I don't think so. We've both been extra busy, so sometimes we don't talk as much."

Terry had been getting towels out of the cupboard across from the tub. He raised his eyebrows at me. I shrugged. I supposed Scoobie and I had been a tad more polite to each other this evening. I'd have to tell him to crack some jokes.

GEORGE CAME BACK TO the house with Scoobie after their meeting. He plopped on the couch. "So, word is out someone will be charged with involuntary manslaughter tomorrow."

Terry called from the kitchen. "For Ms. Cartwright?"

"Yep," George said. "But I'm not sure who."

Terry walked through the living room with a two-inch thick sandwich, heading for the stairs. "I better call Kevin."

I looked from George to Scoobie. "Something doesn't feel right."

"No reason for you to snoop?" asked Scoobie.

"You didn't figure it out, so you're ticked," George said.

I bent over to pick up several Legos from under the coffee table. "Neither. It just feels…too perfect."

"Except for Sandra being dead," Scoobie said.

Except for that.

CHAPTER SEVENTEEN

WHEN THE COUNTY ATTORNEY filed charges on Thursday against Quentin Wharton for involuntary manslaughter, it was almost a letdown. Tiffany's piece in the *Ocean Alley Press* said that Wharton's car had been seen behind Sandra Cartwright's house the night she was killed. She and Wharton had gotten into an argument when they discussed her refusal to vote to invest some of the hospital endowment fund in the resort.

Though Wharton ultimately admitted to being there and receiving her letter of resignation, he maintained that she was fine when he left her. Angry, but healthy. His attorney entered a not-guilty plea on his client's behalf and said he would issue a statement "at an appropriate time."

The article said, "Statements from insurance representative Peter Clayton pointed police toward Wharton." No mention of Clayton leaving her alone and only being helpful after he determined that Kevin and I would recognize him. I supposed the police wanted to make him appear one-hundred-percent credible. And perhaps he was.

The article did mention that "relevant evidence" had been found in Wharton's home, followed by his angry accusation that the police must have put it there.

What surprised me was that Wharton had been released on a $500,000 bond. He put up his house as collateral and the judge revoked his passport. The hospital placed him on administrative leave, still collecting his salary "at this time."

If Wharton had actually sent Peter Clayton to Sandra's house, I bet the release would worry Clayton. Or even if he hadn't, Clayton had implicated Wharton, who could not be pleased.

FROM THURSDAY FORWARD, OUR free time revolved around Aunt Madge's campaign. With daylight savings time in place, we ate microwave dinners and left the house to distribute campaign literature and talk to folks on the boardwalk until eight o'clock.

Scoobie and I each had a twin in a backpack-like carrier, and they delighted in handing out the flyers. Until Saturday afternoon, when we'd all had enough of being away from home and eating on the fly.

Lance had the first meltdown, closely followed by Leah. I felt bad for leading them to that much frustration.

With both of them lying face down on the living room floor, Scoobie and I hauled out the big box of Legos and started snapping them together. It doesn't matter what we make, the Legos calm the kids in a few minutes.

This time took a little longer, but Lance eventually let Scoobie help him make a firetruck and Leah and I constructed a footbridge. She informed us it ran over a creek, which she wished we had in our yard. I had no idea where that came from.

Before their nap, Scoobie read to them from the worn *Child's Garden of Verses*, the one book that had survived his mother's purge when he was little. They went to sleep to their favorite Robert Louis Stevenson poem, which they call the swing poem. "Up in the air I go flying again. Up in the air and down."

When the refreshed versions of Leah and Lance awoke, Scoobie and I took Terry and the twins to dinner at Arnie's Diner. He doesn't have mac n' cheese on the menu, but he has prepackaged cups of it to heat in the microwave.

We had begun to eat our ice cream desserts when Quentin Wharton walked in, scanned the diner, and then made for our table.

"Scoobie, we're getting company."

Scoobie and Terry followed my gaze, and Terry said, "Isn't that the bigwig from the hospital? The man who got arrested?"

"Yes," we both said.

Leah spoke to no one in particular, "Daddy works at the hospital."

Wharton stopped next to us. "Can I sit for a minute? I won't be long."

I said, "For a minute" and Scoobie said, "Sure."

Wharton took a chair from another table, and I moved my chair toward Lance. That meant Wharton couldn't move as close to the table as he perhaps intended.

Terry placed his spoon back in his ice cream bowl and stared at Wharton.

"What do you want?" I asked.

"I didn't kill Sandra Cartwright."

"Respectfully," Scoobie said, "we have nothing to do with police or prosecuting attorney decisions."

Wharton turned slightly to face me. "My lawyer has been talking to the prosecuting attorney staff about why I was arrested. They said Peter Clayton claimed I told him to go there the night Sandra was murdered, to see if she was dead. I didn't."

"Why are you here?" Scoobie asked.

Lance picked up a mac 'n cheese noodle from the table and handed it to Terry. "This is dirty."

"Thanks, buddy," Terry said.

"You're welcome, bub," Lance said.

The childish chatter made us all relax. "Lance," Scoobie said, "you have more ice cream in your bowl."

Leah had continued to eat steadily. She looked in her bowl. "Mine is almost all gone."

Wharton looked from me to Scoobie. "Someone had to see something that night. That's when Sergeant Morehouse's nephew ran away for a few days. Did he see anything?"

Was he truly unaware that Clayton not only told the police Wharton told him to go there, but that Kevin saw Clayton next to Sandra's house?

Terry said, "I don't think it would be good for you to call Kevin."

Wharton shook his head firmly. "I would not. And I've been told not to."

Scoobie and I exchanged glances. I said, "I'm not sure we can…"

"My lawyer also said that Jolie and Sergeant Morehouse's nephew saw someone on the boardwalk during your fundraiser. There was a 9-1-1 call."

I hadn't forgotten about the boardwalk call, but I also hadn't thought that it would so readily tie Kevin and me to Peter Clayton. "I don't know that I can really…"

"You've got to help me Jolie." His voice broke, and he lowered it. "I didn't kill Sandra."

The twins seemed to realize the conversation was now serious. They stared at Wharton.

Arnie's voice came from behind me. "You guys have everything you need?"

I thought the question meant, "Are you okay?"

Scoobie nodded at Arnie. "We're good for now. Thanks, Arnie."

My eyes met Terry's for a moment. His face didn't betray any thoughts. I looked at Wharton. "I don't feel in a position to answer your question, but if your attorney learned about the 9-1-1 call, he can surely ask the police who Kevin and I saw on the boardwalk."

Terry's head turned sharply toward me.

"You want my daddy to get you ice cream?" Leah asked.

Wharton's smile appeared genuine. "I'll get some later." He turned to Scoobie. "I'm sorry I barged in. I'm just so desperate. No one will help me."

Scoobie nodded slowly. "I…don't know that we can help you immediately, but we'll certainly reserve judgment until we've heard all the facts."

We will?

Wharton stood. He seemed calmer. "Thank you." He walked out of the diner.

When he was gone, Terry glared at us. "Why did you even talk to him?"

Scoobie shrugged. "The alternative would have been to ask Arnie to send him away, and that didn't seem right."

Terry said nothing, but turned to Lance to encourage him to finish his ice cream.

I looked directly at Scoobie. "Considering Wharton had to have a hand in that letter you got, I bet you never expected him to ask us for help."

"He's asking you. I don't feel threatened, but we better let Morehouse know."

Given Morehouse's penchant for telling me to butt out, quite loudly sometimes, after we put the twins to bed, we called Dana Johnson.

She listened without saying anything, then asked, "Did you feel endangered in any way?"

With the phone on speaker, we both said no. I added, "He seemed desperate, but it could have all been an act."

"And you didn't tell him Peter Clayton is who you saw on the boardwalk, or why that was important to Kevin?" she asked.

"No." Scoobie said.

I added, "I would have expected him to know it."

"My assumption is that he'll know soon enough." Dana paused. "From what I hear, the initial decision not to share that was based on concern for Kevin's safety.

Very few people know you and he think a car tried to hit him. But I expect word will get around."

From the door to the hallway, Terry said, "I think Kevin even told some people."

Dana sighed. "No one asked him not to. I'm sure it's a...vivid memory for him."

Terry shrugged and turned to mount the stairs.

I raised my eyebrows at Scoobie. "Dana, can I ask you a question?"

Scoobie rolled his eyes at me.

Dana's tone belied humor. "Sure, you can ask."

"Are you one-hundred-percent positive Wharton did it? Is there DNA evidence or something?"

"Prosecuting Attorney Milner must be sure, or she wouldn't have filed charges. Crimes were solved in New Jersey for hundreds of years before we had DNA evidence, and it does take time to test and compare samples. Labs can easily take a month or much longer."

I persisted. "But if Wharton says he didn't do it, what makes you so sure?"

"Most suspects claim innocence. He was initially pretty cagey during his interviews with us. He later admitted he went to her house, they argued, and he left. When suspects switch stories, it makes them a lot less credible."

"So that's it?" I asked.

"There's more, but it's not up to me to tell you. Your information made it clear Clayton and Wharton knew each other, had a business relationship. Wharton was known to be angry with Ms. Cartwright. Even though Kevin saw Clayton, he didn't have a history with her, and Clayton had no clear motive." Dana cleared her throat. "You've never been loose-lipped after we talk, but I really shouldn't discuss this more."

We hung up and Scoobie stared at me. "Feeling guilty?"

I DIDN'T EXACTLY FEEL guilty, but I thought it possible that my willingness to believe Peter Clayton may have made his statements more believable to the police. He was friendly. I liked the guy.

If Sandra had used her fingernails to scratch her killer, should the police have waited for that evidence to be processed before they arrested Wharton? Was it at least partially my fault that they didn't?

Sunday we didn't go to church. We thought the twins had had enough crowd interaction to last a week or more.

Since the temperature hovered near seventy, we drove to the beach and let the kids play in the sand. The breeze from the ocean was still chilly enough that Lance and Leah had no interest in walking by the water. They also didn't like wearing their beach hats, but we kept plopping them back on their heads.

Beaches at the Jersey shore don't have as much sand between the boardwalk and ocean as they did when I was a kid, but there's still plenty of room to sunbathe and play. Scoobie and I sat on a blanket while Lance dug holes and Leah looked for shells.

"I know what you're thinking," he said.

I smiled. "Hard to let go after Wharton's request. But I can't think of what else to do."

Scoobie grunted and nodded to our right. "Maybe you and George can put your heads together."

George and Ramona ambled toward us. The weather was warm enough for George to be in one of his Hawaiian-style shirts and khaki shorts. Ramona wore a pair of lightweight capris with a loose-fitting top. Since she rarely wears anything but dresses, I wondered what had made her go for pants.

"You actually asked George to talk to me about the arrest?"

Scoobie shrugged. "You like to talk capers with someone. I don't. But something about Wharton's protestations bothered me."

"Hi, you two," Ramona said. She handed George half of the blanket she carried under her arm, and they spread it next to ours.

I tried not to smirk at George, who was deliberately not meeting my eyes.

I turned to Ramona as they sat next to us. "I haven't seen final numbers, but I think your booth made almost $700 for Harvest for All."

"I heard that. Cost me less than twenty-five dollars in supplies. I should do it more often."

"Thanks." I looked around her to George. "Did Scoobie tell you what's up?"

From about thirty feet away, Lance yelled, "Hey George, come dig!"

"In a few minutes, buddy."

Lance held up his bucket of sand. "I'll save you a hole!"

Ramona laughed. She did that a lot lately.

George took off his sandals and brushed sand from then. "So, you think Quentin Wharton is innocent?"

"I believe he was there that night to try to convince her to sway the Endowment Committee to invest in the resort, that he and Sandra argued, and she handed him a letter of resignation, which probably made him even more angry. After that, I guess I need help piecing it together."

Scoobie shook his head slightly. "Because the police can't?"

Ramona stood. "Come on, Scoobie, let's help Leah hunt for shells."

He looked at me and grumbled. "You're trying to get rid of me."

I smiled. "I'm not, Ramona is."

They called to Lance and Leah and joined the twins for a stroll down the beach.

I grinned at George. "Nice date."

"Stuff it. After Scoobie called, I thought a lot about it. You kind of have to look at it in two pieces. One is the murder itself, and the other is who benefits."

I nodded. "And the third piece is who seemingly followed me when I looked for Kevin and tried to knock him over with their car, maybe even kill him."

George watched Ramona walk away from us. "And we make the assumption that the driver of that car felt threatened by Kevin in some way, but we don't think it was this guy Clayton, whom Kevin saw in Sandra's driveway. Right?"

George shaded his eyes to watch a sailboat skidding across the water not far from shore. "Could have been the killer behind the wheel, could have been someone the killer hired. And Wharton and Clayton are possibilities."

"It doesn't make sense that Clayton would come to the fundraiser to be sure Kevin or I saw him, and then show up at the house I was appraising. Would a guilty person do that?"

"Could be as simple as finding out if you or Terry recognized him. Or maybe to create a different narrative."

George's gaze strayed back to Ramona. "Otherwise, the only story is that Kevin saw a man leaving Sandra's place apparently not long after someone killed her, and that man was Peter Clayton."

"You've known her since high school. Now you have to examine her back every two minutes." He glared at me and I smirked. "I guess not her back."

"Stuff it! You want to talk about this, right?"

I nodded. "I keep coming back to what was so important about investing that money. A few days ago, Wharton told me he'd been interested in working as the resort CEO, but he decided against trying for it because, basically, Borman is an SOB."

George frowned. "Little detail I don't remember you telling me."

"Since it seems a number of people think Borman's a jerk, it kind of made sense. What if Wharton getting that job depended on him getting the Endowment Committee to invest…I don't even know how much."

"According to their last annual report, the committee oversees assets of almost twelve million dollars. Not that it would all be liquid."

I had been leaning back on my elbows on our blanket, but sat up straighter. "Wow! Why didn't I ever think to look into that?"

George shrugged. "Public info, but since it didn't look as if any money would go to Borman's resort, I didn't dig into it until yesterday."

The wind blew a little harder, and I pulled more sunscreen from my beach bag. "I should put more on the kids. Windburn is easy to get."

"Your nose is getting sunburned. You can get the twins in a minute."

Scoobie, Ramona, and the twins were several hundred yards from us, but had stopped walking. From the poking Lance did with his plastic shovel, I figured they'd come across a dead crab or fish.

"The thing is," I said, "a few million is a drop in the bucket for a big commercial project like that. What difference would it make?"

"Leverage for more, I suppose."

"So maybe Wharton talked to Sandra and, like his attorney said, they argue but she's alive when he leaves."

George shrugged. "And for some reason Wharton calls Clayton to go to Sandra's to what...kill her to eliminate her no vote? That's ludicrous."

"Agreed. But maybe Wharton simply called to tell Clayton that Sandra wouldn't change her mind. He might not have asked Clayton to do anything."

I warmed to my idea. "Maybe Clayton decided on his own to convince Sandra to support investing from the endowment fund. Clayton wanted to encourage her, so he'd get the additional insurance business."

"That's a mouthful." George looked down the beach. "They're coming back."

"I see that. Clayton goes to her place, she knows him, so she lets him in. From the back entrance, where people park, same way Wharton went in."

George smiled. "And he whacks her?"

"Not on purpose. He could have…could have been menacing or something, she backed up and tripped. That would be an accident. The big crime was in not getting her help. Scoobie said she could have lived."

"Yeah. That's what the ME said. But the thing is, the police and Annie Milner must think they have evidence to support what Clayton said, that he went there after Wharton called and found her dead. Hard to drive a wedge in between facts."

"Unless we could find out one of two things. First, who put Sandra's purse in Wharton's house – the man himself or someone who wanted to implicate him? Second, who drove that car that tried to hit Kevin?"

CHAPTER EIGHTEEN

SCOOBIE AND I PUT THE lightly sunburned twins to bed Sunday evening and sat on the couch, feet on the coffee table, holding hands.

"Too much going on," Scoobie said.

"Thanks for inviting George and Ramona to meet us at the beach."

He grinned. "You mean thanks for giving my blessing to you two talking crime solving."

"Excuse me!" I looked at him, noting the smirk on his face. "Oh, you. I am trying not to look into things behind your back."

"I know."

While we ate, I had told him and Terry what George and I talked about. Terry had reaffirmed that Kevin had no idea what kind of car had gone after him. He'd been as blinded by the headlights as I had.

I put my head on Scoobie's shoulder. "I can't think of anything else to do. What if Wharton is innocent and I helped the police think he's guilty?"

"They might start with you kind of vouching for Clayton, but it was up to them to figure out what to do with that."

"I guess I could tell them what George and I talked about."

"You could, or let George do it."

"George doesn't seem to think it's likely Clayton did it. Clayton didn't have as much at stake as Wharton. Assuming Wharton really did want that CEO job. Or, being altruistic, wanted to increase the hospitals patient usage."

Scoobie shook his head slightly. "All we know is Wharton wanted the job with the resort. Borman hasn't said he tied the endowment fund investment to a job offer."

AFTER SCOOBIE LEFT FOR WORK, Monday morning, I ruminated. I couldn't verify private conversations between Jack Borman and Quentin Wharton, or Wharton and Peter Clayton.

What about the conversation Kevin had overhead in the recovery room? If it was between Wharton and Clayton, maybe Morehouse could work on that angle. *Or maybe it was between Borman and Wharton.* I had frustrated myself.

I called Morehouse and outlined my thinking.

"Jolie, you think we sit around here with our thumbs in our ears?"

He didn't have to be rude. "Ears? No. And what about what Kevin heard in the recovery room? Have you asked about…?"

"We know what we have to follow up on. Stay out of it!" He hung up.

I wanted to have the sense of peace that comes from knowing a bad guy has been caught. Maybe I could see if Wharton's or Clayton's cars had a scratch on its front fender.

I dropped off the twins and called George. "Can you look up where Peter Clayton lives, and whether he has a car besides the red VW he drove to Ocean Alley last week?"

"Jolie, I don't mind talking to you about this, but I've got a new contract to do background checks for a big car dealer that has locations in Lakewood and Asbury Park and a couple other places."

"Why do they need background checks for car sellers?"

"What they told me is because the sales staff take people for test drives, and they want to know who they're putting with their customers. Probably more about liability."

Feeling out of sorts, I said, "Maybe they should check the buyers. They could be anybody."

He laughed. "Call me in a couple days. I want to get a few of these done quickly, so they know how good I am."

"I'll be sure to tell Ramona."

"Stuff it."

I smiled as I hung up. Aloud I said, "It would be so much fun if they stayed together."

The warm temperature and blue sky made me wish Scoobie and the kids and I were strolling on the boardwalk instead of me stopping by the appraisal office. No new work, but because the Internet is faster, I stuck around.

I knew where Quentin Wharton's house was. My goal was to see where Peter Clayton lived. He had said between Ocean Alley and Lakewood.

I learned that his independent insurance agency was in Allenwood, a small town, and he seemed to have a residence on its outskirts. Google Maps indicated he lived in a cluster of three houses, situated on about an acre. The third-acre lots looked small, and Google Earth showed much of the area was wooded.

Since it was only nine A.M., I had plenty of time to drive there, see if I could find a car besides the Volkswagen, go to the grocery store, and get the B&B ready for a possible victory party for Aunt Madge the next night.

Harry had the idea for the party. My role was to clean the first floor well and hide a lot of snack food in a third-floor guest room. We could retrieve it and put up streamers when results were known. Harry seemed pretty confident she would win.

I couldn't envision Aunt Madge as the Ocean Alley mayor, but a few years ago I couldn't have imagined me married to Scoobie and the mother of twins. What did I know?

The drive to Allenwood took less than thirty minutes. The town was pretty, but no ocean breeze. I never wanted to live away from the ocean again. I pushed aside the thought that someone might be trying to get Scoobie fired. It couldn't possibly happen.

Peter Clayton's bungalow was not shabby, but it didn't reflect a lot of TLC. The lawn was groomed but not really landscaped, and the house had older aluminum siding rather than wood or newer vinyl siding.

Behind the house was a one-car, detached garage with its door open. In fact, it didn't appear to have a door. The garage did not hold the VW. The insignia on the back of the car parked there was that of a Toyota, I thought an older Camry. I had Toyotas for years.

My original Corolla had not had the brighter headlights, but my sister had a newer one with the garish LED lights. I don't like them because they're too intense. *Just like the car with the scratch.*

I parked my car a couple hundred yards from Clayton's driveway. None of the houses looked as if their residents were home. Probably at work.

My clipboard sat on my passenger seat. I wasn't doing an appraisal, but I certainly knew how to look as if I was supposed to be prowling the exterior of a home.

With my camera resting on the clipboard, I pushed aside my inclination to creep around the house. I took one photo from the end of the driveway, and started walking with a purposeful stride toward the garage. I stopped twice to make imaginary notations on my clipboard.

I peered into the garage from a few feet away from it. Too dark to see much other than dark walls and some gardening tools on a shelf. My phone would have to serve as a flashlight.

Better to move quickly. I walked into the garage and to the front of the car. I placed my clipboard and camera on the car's hood, and unlocked my phone so that its screen light was fully luminous.

Although I might not have picked out the car's scratch from a geometric lineup, it looked the same as the one I had stared at for several seconds as it came toward Kevin. I used my phone's camera to take a picture.

A man's voice came from the rear of the car. "Jolie, what the hell are you doing here?"

Startled, I dropped the phone. "Oh, um, just checking something. I might, uh, apply at an appraisal firm in Allenwood."

"The hell you say." He moved to the side of the car, coming toward me.

"Yikes!" I moved too, and we stared across the car roof at one another.

Gone was the amiable smile. Peter Clayton radiated fury. "I need that photo."

I took a breath. "I think my phone is just under your car, where I was standing a second ago."

"What do you think you're trying to prove, anyway?"

"Prove? I can't prove anything. I thought maybe I could, uh, get someone to take a look at the scratch on the front of your car. On your bumper."

His words came out as a sneer. "In the market for a used car, are you?"

My mouth felt as dry as sand, and I swallowed. He knew why I was in his garage "No. Just trying to figure out who tried to hit Kevin that night. And maybe why."

"Not me."

"Not you what?" I asked.

"Don't play games."

"I don't think it was ever in the paper that someone came at Kevin after I found him at the salt water taffy place. Shouldn't you be asking me what night, or why I thought someone would try to hit Kevin?"

Great Jolie. See if you can make him angrier.

Clayton stared at me. "Time for you to leave."

Somehow, I didn't think he really meant for me to be able to do that. "How about if you drive away first?"

He shook his head. "You should have stayed away."

"My phone has location software. It'll show I was here."

He smiled thinly. "But by the time someone looks, you won't be. I, of course, never saw you here."

I wished I had stopped at a gas station to go to the bathroom on the way into Allenwood.

"How'd you get so involved in all this, anyway? Was the money you'd make from selling that new insurance really that much?"

"You're nosy."

"Persistent. How much was it?"

Clayton didn't take his eyes off me. "Over time, enough to pay off my house."

"And that made it worth killing Sandra?"

"Accident." Clayton moved a few steps toward the front of the car. I moved a few steps toward the back.

"How did you get her purse into Wharton's house?"

He tightened and then loosened his jaw. "You shouldn't talk so much."

"I've been told…"

Suddenly, he jumped high and began to scramble across the hood.

I screamed and made for the lawn. I cleared the garage and ran down the driveway. Could I get to my car before Clayton caught up to me?

Feet pounded behind me. Clayton was faster, and my slight advantage from leaving the garage ahead of him was almost gone.

His hand brushed my shoulder. My adrenalin kicked up about ten notches and I ran faster. He couldn't get a good hold on me. Yet.

My chest burned. *I'm not going to make it to my car!*

Tires squealed and a car roared up the driveway. George threw his SUV into park and jumped out, holding the tire iron he keeps under his front seat. "You don't want to mess with me, Clayton."

I veered right, ran to George's Highlander, wrenched open the front passenger door, and jumped in. I sat panting, watching the two frozen figures standing about twenty feet apart.

"Jolie," George called. "Open my glove compartment."

I leaned forward and pulled. Sitting on top of the SUV's owner's manual was a gun. In crime novels people know the type of gun and comment on the ammunition or something else. I knew this gun to be black.

I'd never touched a handgun. "Is this yours?"

"No, it's the tooth fairy's. Bring it to me. It won't go off."

With my left hand, I pulled it toward me by the handle. *This sucker is heavy!* With my right hand I opened the door and pushed it wide open with my foot. I stood up. "Okay, bringing it to you."

For a second I thought Clayton would move toward George, but he held the tire iron like a baseball bat. "Come on over."

Clayton stayed still, breathing hard.

From down the road, police sirens roared toward us. Perhaps one of the neighbors had been home after all.

"Put the gun back, Jolie. I'll show them I have it."

"You do have a license, right?"

Still looking at Clayton, George smiled grimly. "Private investigators don't leave home without one."

MOREHOUSE EXPLAINED TO THE Monmouth County Sheriff that George and I were not criminals, just criminally nosy. It didn't make our questioning go any faster, but it probably made it marginally less unpleasant. It also helped me not get arrested for trespassing. I probably could have been.

We had been allowed to drive our cars to the police station. When the police let us leave, George and I stood together in the parking lot before we drove back to Ocean Alley.

"Thanks, George."

He shook his head. "I was driving to Lakewood and had this insane idea that you might look for Clayton's car on your own. If I hadn't believed you could be so irrational, you could be dead."

I sighed. "I'm sure I'll hear that a lot the next few days."

"Did you call Scoobie?"

"I called Harry and asked him to call him."

George laughed. "What a chicken."

"Listen, I hate to ask…"

"What?"

"Are you going to put a lock on that glove compartment?"

"When I saw how nimble Lance was with his sand shovel, I ordered a special safe for my car trunk. Should get it in a few days. Don't want the twins to find it, but I could need to have the gun with me sometimes."

I grinned. "I was worried about you shooting yourself in the foot. Literally, this time."

"Next time I'll keep driving to Lakewood."

I glanced at my watch. "I'm supposed to buy groceries for Aunt Madge's surprise victory party tomorrow night."

"You okay to drive home?"

"Yes. What do you think happens now?"

George shrugged. "To us, probably nothing. I'd say Morehouse and Tortino have their work cut out for them."

I nodded, wishing it were tomorrow, because everyone would be a little less angry with me. Probably.

"If I were you, I'd buy Scoobie flowers."

CHAPTER NINETEEN

IT'S A GOOD DAY WHEN you know your husband won't leave you no matter how angry he is. He did like the flowers, a mix of multi-colored carnations and roses.

I don't think of myself as a sleuth, just a concerned person. But knowing the right person would be charged with Sandra's death was definitely a good feeling. Dropping off the kids at daycare and thinking of little more than doing an appraisal and picking up surprise party goodies were also good.

I gave myself the luxury of sitting in Java Jolt Tuesday morning to drink coffee and read the paper. The editor had asked George to write the article questioning who killed Sandra Cartwright – based on new information.

He mentioned that "some people" were angry with her because she would not support investing hospital endowment funds in the resort. George avoided saying that Borman may have made securing the money an important part of developing the resort. My guess was we would start to hear about more requests from Shoreline Investments to local firms.

For the first time since everything started, the paper covered the car that attempted to hit Kevin. The article then described my connecting it to Clayton, though "as yet there is no information on who was behind the wheel." Ocean Alley Police were directing questions about Clayton's car to Monmouth County.

Bottom line, Prosecuting Attorney Milner was reconsidering charges to file against Quentin Wharton. I figured he'd at least be accused of obstructing the investigation. What was not yet certain was whether he asked Clayton to go talk to Sandra or if Clayton, wanting a big commission, went on his own.

I said goodbye to Megan and headed to the courthouse. My phone chirped as I entered the building, and Sergeant Morehouse's name appeared on caller ID. "Hi, Sergeant, or should I say Matthew?"

"What you should say is you'll butt out of police business."

Irritation welled. Hadn't I just helped figure out Quentin Wharton probably didn't kill Sandra Cartwright? "Excuse me?"

"We got the print results from that letter we found under Sandra's blotter." When I said nothing, he added, "Don't you want to say 'what letter'?"

"I suppose I could."

"There bein' no prints at all, not even hers, means someone else looked at it and probably made that copy, wearin' gloves. I think I'm talking to that someone."

I decided not to throw Lester under the bus. "I figured you'd be mad that I touched it, and you'd find it in a few minutes anyway."

"Knowing potential motive matters, and delay could keep a killer on the street. You do that kind of bunk again and those cute twins'll be visiting you behind bars!" He hung up.

I thought being jailed was unlikely at any point, but Morehouse had certainly put a damper on my day.

I unlocked the door to the appraisal office and checked the fax machine as soon as I'd placed my purse on my desk. No new Lester requests.

Uh oh. I should have called Lester to tell him about my run-in with Clayton. Lester got Morehouse to let us into Sandra's house under false pretenses. If we hadn't been able to do that, I would not have found the copy of Sandra's resignation letter. That letter made me realize Wharton could have been even angrier with her than I had thought.

I called Lester.

"Oh, Jolie Gentil. I know that dame. I thought she forgot her buddy Lester."

"Jolie got herself in trouble and had her phone taken away."

Lester barked his laugh, but he didn't sound like he thought anything was funny. "And George rescued you? How'd he know you were there?"

"He, uh, decided I was crazy enough to look for Clayton's car, and followed a hunch."

"You owe me coffee for a month." Lester hung up.

I thought I got off easy. He could have asked me to support the price on one of his more ludicrous sales.

Even though there were fewer than ten hours before we'd know if Aunt Madge would be the next mayor of Ocean Alley, I still had work to do.

I collected information I needed to conduct the appraisal visit at one of the ritzy houses on the north side of town. Usually those went to our competitors at Stenner Appraisal. We were a little cheaper. My father used to say rich people got that way by saving pennies.

The property owner turned out to be Hardin Grooms, a current member of the city council. We had worked together on the first election campaign of the county's Prosecuting Attorney, Annie Milner, more than five years ago. I wondered where Grooms stood on the resort.

I called Aunt Madge at the Cozy Corner. "Is Hardin Grooms someone you're in cahoots with?"

"Actually, I think he's on the fence about the resort. At least he won't say if he's made up his mind. Why do you ask?"

"I'm heading over to his place to appraise it."

"That's…odd," she said. "I haven't heard he's moving away."

"Aren't he and his wife close to sixty? Maybe they're downsizing."

"Could be." Her cell phone rang in the background. "Please be on your best behavior."

I looked at my now quiet cell phone. "I behave." *Mostly*.

I studied the front of the residence for a minute after I pulled up. Two stories, pale blue vinyl siding over the prior frame construction, yellow shutters, and a beautifully manicured lawn. With sandy soil throughout much of town, I bet they'd had a lot of topsoil brought in.

Hardin opened the door himself. "I hoped it would be you instead of Harry."

At my questioning look, he laughed. "I wanted to see how Madge's campaign is going. He's her manager, so all he'll tell me is great."

I entered the large foyer and glanced up the center-hall steps. Almost majestic. "I don't think they're doing polls or anything. She's been getting more invitations to speak to groups."

He shut the door. "Sandra's death, now the council hears talk about Borman asking local businesses to invest. Some people are rethinking their support for it."

How about you? "I'd love to have more hotel rooms, but I'd rather see them in smaller chunks."

Grooms nodded. "I'm kind of coming to that conclusion, too. We'd have to give Borman's resort some tax incentives, then the town would lose a fair bit of property tax revenue from the businesses they might buy out for space to build. Plus, there'd be a lot of street work to do."

I took my notebook and measuring tape from my purse. "And I'd hate to lose Mr. Markle's grocery."

When Grooms offered to show me around, I said I'd work faster alone, if he didn't mind. He picked car keys off a table by the door. "I hoped you'd say that. I have a lot of reading to do before tomorrow's council meeting. Just make sure the front doorknob is locked when you leave."

As soon as he pulled out of his driveway I called Aunt Madge. "I think you have an ally."

"Ah, good. He and one other member haven't come down either way. We may win that council vote yet."

I have a lot of confidence in Aunt Madge. To be honest with myself, I didn't anticipate people electing a mayor in her eighties, but I could see her doing the job.

Then I felt guilty because if she won I would have lots more afternoon teas to serve. *Stop being selfish.*

AFTER LUNCH, I STOPPED AT the Cozy Corner to drop off an ice cream cake I'd ordered for the party. For a change, Aunt Madge sat at her kitchen table. She acted as if me putting an ice cream cake in her freezer was an everyday occurrence.

I placed my hand on her forehead. "You aren't campaigning?"

"Harry and I decided we would rest on the big day." She stood to put her teacup into the sink. "I'm still mad at you."

"I'm mad at me, too. I didn't think it was dangerous, but I took a big risk going up there."

She stood, hands on hips, to regard me. She never stands like that. "Okay, that's good. You're trainable."

"Where's Harry? At the office?"

"I think he's out getting things for the party."

"Oh, I thought that was a surprise."

She shrugged. "It is. Don't tell him I know."

I grinned. "You want to be a lady of leisure and go to Java Jolt for lunch?"

"Can't. I'm busy."

The quiet of her great room did not support her statement. "Doing what?"

She pointed to the sliding doors and walked to them. The dogs and Jazz sat quietly on the back porch, watching a teenager paint the side of Aunt Madge's garage.

"Who is that boy, and why is Jazz here?"

Aunt Madge blew a kiss to Miss Piggy. "Jazz is here because she roamed from window to window in your house, trying to see what was going on back here. I decided your curtains would be in better shape if I brought her over here."

"Thanks." I pointed to the boy. "You hired him to paint the wood you replaced after the fire?"

"That's Paul Holley's nephew."

My head jerked from the view outside to Aunt Madge. "He started the fire?"

"He lives with Paul and his wife. His father has severe PTSD after service in Afghanistan. The boy, James Holley, was mixed up about how to best help Paul. He was apparently trying to scare me into backing out."

I stared at the James' back as he painted. "How'd you find out?"

"Yesterday he told Paul that he really wanted him to win. He then said what he did to help. Paul called me."

"Wow. Will you call the police?"

She shook her head. "He needs more positive adults in his life, not a serious legal situation." She grinned. "I told Paul that's how we treat people in close-knit communities."

"Subtle." We turned to go back to the table. "Is he, uh, safe to have around?"

"I believe so. He quite likes the dogs. More important, they seem to like him. He's going to stop by from time to time to do some chores for me."

I remembered Jazz breathing hard the night of the fire, as if she had run after someone. "Is he good to Jazz?"

"Now that was odd. She really hissed at him. Miss Piggy had to reprimand her."

I laughed. "Reprimand her?"

"She nudged Jazz toward the B&B a couple of times. Eventually she sat on Mister Rogers' back for a while and calmed down."

I didn't offer my theory about Jazz chasing James. She's very protective, but most people don't believe cats are like that.

WITH EXAMS COMING UP, Terry had no track practice. When I got home, he was sitting at the living room table with a pile of books.

"I'm heading over to get the twins at daycare in a few, if you want to come. I think they want to show you a bunch of new drawings on the bulletin board."

He smiled slightly. "After exams."

When he said nothing else, I began to cut up a head of broccoli and pour ranch dressing into a bowl for the kids' afternoon snack. When he still hadn't said anything as I was almost ready to go, I sat down across from him. "Everything okay?"

He finally flashed a grin. "Mostly good, but I figured you could give me some advice."

"That's a switch. It's usually Scoobie."

He grabbed a bottle of water from the fridge and sat, facing me. "So, Kevin and Cathy Giacomo broke up before all the stuff. You knew that, right?"

"I remember you saying she was mad at him. You think it's permanent?"

He looked toward the backyard and back to me. "I'm thinking of asking her out. You think that's fair?"

"To Kevin, you mean?"

"Yeah. I mean, he's my best friend."

Terry had never asked me such an important question. I didn't want to mess up. "I think it's good you consider Kevin's feelings, but don't you think Cathy can make up her mind on her own?"

"Yeah, and I think she likes me. The first couple days Kevin was missing, we spent a lot of time together looking for him."

That explains why he didn't need so many rides from us. And probably why he's been on the phone a lot lately.

I nodded. "Kevin's been back for a few days. Has he talked to you about making up with her?"

He shrugged. "Not really. I think he might even be waiting for her to say something."

"Was she the one who acted kind of…off?"

Terry grunted. "Nope. He just stopped talking to her."

I twirled the pepper shaker that always sits on our table. "If tomorrow Kevin walked down the hall holding hands with Cathy, how would you feel?"

"Like I really blew it."

I grinned. "I think you just answered your own question."

I STOPPED BY THE In-Town Grocery before I went to vote.

Mr. Markle nodded at me from his spot at the cash register. "Afternoon, Jolie. Hearing a lot of people saying they're voting for Madge."

I walked to him and leaned against the conveyor. "Soon we'll know."

He leaned against the register. "You want her to win?"

"Life would be different, but if she wants it, I want it."

He grinned at me.

I squinted at him. "Okay, you have some kind of good news."

"Borman rescinded his offer. I'm not selling."

"That's great! I mean, you seem fine with it."

He nodded. "It's like that old saying with the penny. As soon as you flip it you know which side you want it to land on. I didn't really want to sell, but turning down good money was bugging me. I didn't have to decide."

I wanted to chat, but I also had work to do. "Let me grab some chicken noodle soup, and I'll be right back."

By the time I'd added soup, crackers, and apple juice to my basket, Mr. Markle was straightening the produce aisle. "I'm glad you're pleased about Borman taking back his offer."

"I've got a few more years to work. Just as soon do it here."

"And we need those bent cans."

THE TWINS WERE IN FULL antic mode when I picked them up at two-forty-five. With a serious face, Lance asked, "Guess what?"

"What?"

"Chicken butt." He and Leah dissolved into fits of laughter, doubled over in their car seats.

I've learned smiling is good, but if I laugh too hard I hear a joke for a week. "Where did you hear that?"

"Lance thought of it," Leah said.

I glanced in the rearview mirror. Lance's knitted brow said he had told her that but was trying to decide if he should tell me something different.

He punted. "What else rhymes with butt?"

"What about shut?" Leah asked.

"That's good. What do you call a small house? A really small one."

That stumped them for almost minute. "Lester sells small houses. You could ask him," Lance said.

I grinned. "Keep trying."

In the mirror, I saw Leah sounding out words. "I know. I know. A small house is a hut!"

"Very good. Now what about…"

"What's smut?" Lance asked.

Oh, good. "Where'd you hear that word?"

Leah answered. "Monica said her mom got rid of smut magazines she found under her brother's bed."

I sighed. "It just means Monica's mom didn't like what he was reading."

"What was he reading?" Lance asked.

Please let distraction work. "When Daddy gets home, you can take the dogs for a walk today."

"Let's go to the park," Leah said.

"No, the corner where we can count trucks," Lance countered.

I let them battle that for the next couple of minutes. When we got near the house, Scoobie pulled into the driveway ahead of me. *Whew*.

He came over to help me unload the kids. Leah gave him a sloppy kiss and handed him a broken red crayon. At least it hadn't melted in her car seat.

"Daddy," Lance said, "we're talking to Mommy about smut."

Scoobie's broad grin didn't require words.

WITH THE TWINS FINALLY sleeping, Scoobie and I planned to change clothes and go to the courthouse with Aunt Madge and Harry to watch election returns. Terry said he'd heard enough about campaigns, so we didn't need to pay for a sitter.

For a change, I was ready before Scoobie. I heard him upstairs talking to Terry, and wondered if Terry had asked him the same question he'd put to me earlier today.

I straightened a pile of the kids' books that sat next to the couch and found a small piece of broccoli next to the toy box. On top of the closed box was a piece of white copy paper.

Studying can help in the test of life.
Success can be measured in lack of strife.
Is it who you are or what you do?
It's about who you love, I know that, too.
Scoobie

I swallowed and reached for a tissue to blow my nose. *I am so lucky.* I placed the paper back on the box for now.

Scoobie ran lightly down the steps and sat on the couch. He patted a spot next to him, and I crossed the room to sit there. We leaned back, holding hands, and placed our feet on the coffee table.

After about a minute of sitting with our eyes closed, recharging, I traced the side of his cheek. "Thank you for the poem."

He opened his eyes and stared at the ceiling. "I still can't believe you'd risk what we have, but I know you don't see it that way."

"I didn't, but I'll be more careful."

He turned his head to me. "Did you almost say 'next time?'"

I laughed. "I did not."

We were quiet again, until I said, "It's been a heck of a couple weeks, hasn't it?"

He nodded. "I think it's ending okay. And my wife is even alive." He stood and walked to the backpack he used for work and removed a piece of folded paper.

I took it. The copy of Scoobie's letter of reprimand had the word 'rescinded' written across it in large, red letters.

My eyes began to tear. "How?"

He sat next to me and took the paper back. "Sam gave it to me. I guess he pushed it with human resources, said if there were a couple of complaints he wanted to see them. Suddenly no one could find them."

I wiped away a tear. "So, you won't have to look for a job?"

"Nope. Ocean Alley is our home as long as we want it to be."

I didn't realize how much I dreaded the possibly of having to leave until the feeling vanished.

I leaned over and kissed him. "The next mayor will be happy about that, too."

BOOKS BY ELAINE L. ORR

Elaine's books are generally self-published, via Lifelong Dreams Publishing. The books are on all e retailer sites, and can be ordered by your local bookstore or library. Most books are in ebooks, paperbacks, large print version, and audio books. Thanks for your interest!

Jolie Gentil Cozy Mystery Series
Appraisal for Murder
Rekindling Motives
When the Carny Comes to Town
Any Port in a Storm
Trouble on the Doorstep
Behind the Walls
Vague Images
Ground to a Halt
Holidays in Ocean Alley
The Unexpected Resolution
Underground in Ocean Alley
Jolie and Scoobie High School Misadventures (prequel)

River's Edge Mystery Series
(Annie Acorn Publishing)
From Newsprint to Footprints
Demise of a Devious Neighbor
Demise of a Devious Suspect (summer 2018)

Logland Mystery Series
Tip a Hat to Murder

http://www.elaineorr.com

ABOUT ELAINE L. ORR

Elaine L. Orr is the Amazon bestselling author of the Jolie Gentil cozy mystery series. *Behind the Walls* was a finalist for the 2014 Chanticleer Mystery and Mayhem Awards. The first book in her River's Edge series, *From Newsprint to Footprints*, came out in late 2015, and the Logland series began with *Tip a Hat to Murder* in 2016. *Demise of a Devious Neighbor*, the second River's Edge book, was a Chanticleer finalist in 2017.

She also writes plays and novellas, including the one-act play, *Common Ground* published in 2015. Her novella, *Falling into Place*, tells the story of a family managing the results of an Iowa father's World War II experience with humor and grace. Another novella, *Biding Time*, was one of five finalists in the National Press Club's first fiction contest, in 1993.

Elaine conducts presentations and teaches online classes on book publishing and other writing-related topics. Nonfiction includes *Writing in Retirement: Putting New Year's Resolutions to Work*, and *Words to Write By: Getting Your Thoughts on Paper*. Elaine grew up in Maryland and moved to the Midwest in 1994.

She graduated from the University of Dayton and the American University. She took fiction courses from The Writer's Center in Bethesda, MD, the University of Iowa Summer Writing Festival, and Georgetown University's Continuing Education Program. Elaine is a regular attendee at Magna Cum Murder. She is a member of Sisters in Crime and the Indiana Writers' Center.

CPSIA information can be obtained
at www.ICGtesting.com
Printed in the USA
LVHW03s0025260818
588169LV00030B/963/P

9 781948 070096